MISSISSIPPI MOONSHINE

KIRSTEN S. BLACKETER

DEDICATION

My husband, who gave me the spark of inspiration for this story.
Kirsten, Christina, and Heather, who beta read for me.
Thank you for your input.
Melissa...my proofer. Your comments make me grin like a fool.
Thank you for those.

TABLE OF CONTENTS

CHAPTER ONE

Alton, Illinois
May 1933

Nathaniel stepped out of the car, tucking his keys into his pocket next to his .38 Special. He strolled along the docks while his gaze scanned the various barges and ships harbored there. The narrow street was lined with vendors selling fresh catfish and buffalo carp caught that morning in the Illinois and Mississippi Rivers. Catfish made his stomach churn. Even the smell of the vile bottom feeding vermin nauseated him. He'd tried it once, and that had been enough to keep him from ever eating it again. Nathaniel turned his head away from the booth.

A body collided with his. Out of instinct, he snatched the arm of the teenager who struggled to right himself. He knew pickpockets with more grace and finesse than this one. Nathaniel patted his wallet with his free hand, then narrowed his eyes on the youth in his grip.

"Let me go!" an unmistakably feminine voice snapped.

He arched a brow as he knocked the cap off the offender's head. A tumble of gold-streaked auburn hair fell from beneath it in a mass of snarls.

Nathaniel smirked. "Well, you're certainly a surprise. What's your name, kid?"

"Go to hell, ya limey bastard!" She snarled as she struggled to pull from his grip.

The girl was a feisty little thing with a dirty mouth. Certainly not a lady. He eyed her small figure and bright features beneath the dirt smudged face and the atrocious mess of her tangled hair. *But she had the potential. Delicate and spirited.* Worst of all, she intrigued him. *A dangerous prospect indeed.*

"Are you here alone, kid?" he asked while forcing a polite smile.

"Stop calling me that, you pompous jackass, and let me go before I call a copper!" She lunged for him, baring her teeth.

"Damn it, Ginny! Have you lost all control of your senses?" a new voice chimed in as a tall man stepped from the shadows of the alley. "Apologize right now!" he demanded, scowling at the young woman.

"He's the one who should be apologizing. See the way he's manhandling me?" She huffed, gesturing to his hand on her arm.

Nathaniel released her and straightened his lapels. "Please accept my apologies, miss. I had no idea a foul-mouthed girl existed beneath those rags."

Her jaw dropped open. He merely smiled.

"I'm so sorry, mister," the man said, taking ahold of the girl's hand. "My sister didn't mean to be so rude."

"I most certainly did." She snorted. "He wasn't watchin' where he was goin' and he ran straight into me."

"I beg your pardon, miss." Nathaniel bowed slightly. "If you'll excuse me."

He pushed past the pair and continued down the street. With one last glance over his shoulder, he saw the defiant hellion watching him with an eagle eye. Although he couldn't explain it, somehow he knew their paths would cross again.

The steam ship lay just ahead. The *Mississippi Queen* had seen better days, but she fared well on the trips he required of her. Her stacks rose above the buildings in the harbor, making her easy to spot from his location. He'd stop there before visiting Mr. Chapman's farm.

He refocused his attention from the hellion to the business matters at hand. Secure the shipment and speak to

Mr. Chapman about the next order.

The captain stood on the gangplank talking to one of the workers loading supplies onto the ship. With Levi at the helm, Nathaniel could rest assured his shipments would remain safe and reach their destination. Their ten-year friendship had weathered more than he cared to remember. Levi proved the most trustworthy captain on the river, with an intimate knowledge of her waterways.

When Levi caught sight of Nathaniel he dismissed the deckhand and made his way toward the gangplank.

"Levi." Nathaniel shook his friend's hand and glanced up at the ship. "When will she be ready to shove off?"

"No time for pleasantries, eh, Blackthorne?" He thrust his hands in his coat pockets.

Levi had grown his dark hair out as soon as they were released from the army. He wore it long, tied back with a faded ribbon. His beard had filled in since Nathaniel had seen him last. The man looked more like a pirate with every passing day. How fitting.

"We'll be ready to go by tomorrow evening. My men have a few other shipments to load, including yours." He narrowed his gaze at Nathaniel.

"The crates will be delivered this evening after sunset. I'm on my way to meet with Chapman."

The sunlight glinted high in the sky before disappearing behind a fluffy white cloud. He squinted against the light.

"Looks like we'll have fair weather for the trip. I hope you don't have an aversion to my accompanying the shipment to Baton Rouge."

Levi shook his head. "None, as long as you keep your part of the arrangement and leave a case for me."

"You'll be well compensated for any and all risks. You always are." Nathaniel smiled at his friend's businesslike tone. "I shall return tonight to be sure the cargo is stored properly."

"You don't trust me?" the captain asked.

"I wouldn't let you haul my booze if I didn't." Nathaniel shook his head.

"True." Levi chuckled. "I'll leave your cabin open then." He turned with a nod and resumed inventory on the cargo waiting to be loaded. "Care for a hand or two tonight?"

"I thought you quit gambling." Nathaniel stared at his friend. "One of these days I won't be around to bail you out."

"It's just a friendly game of poker between friends." Levi winked before turning. "The offer stands," he called over his shoulder.

Nathaniel shook his head and flipped open his pocket watch. *Just after twelve-thirty.* It gave him enough time to meet with Mr. Chapman before supper. He strode back to his car, parked just outside the market. As he passed the fish stands, he pulled out his cigarette case and scanned the crowd for the familiar cap concealing the smart-mouthed girl.

He shook his head.

"You're daydreaming about a child. Could you be any more pathetic?" Nathaniel scolded himself under his breath and then pulled out a rolled cigarette. He tucked it between his lips and lit it.

Once he reached his new black Lincoln coupe, he started it, letting the engine purr for a moment before heading for the main street out of the town of Alton.

The small community rested just above Saint Louis where the Illinois and Mississippi Rivers joined. Perfect for hiding and transporting hooch, but it boasted little of the civilities Nathaniel was accustomed to. His predominant business dealings kept him in Baton Rouge and occasionally Saint Louis. But his supplier resided just north of Alton, which made its harbor a safer alternative to transfer his livelihood south.

Levi assured him there were plenty of locations farther south where he could acquire his goods, but Nathaniel had worked with Mr. Chapman from the very beginning. He'd met the man on several occasions, but never before had he seen the farm first hand. All of their business dealings up to this point had been through a solicitor of sorts, who unfortunately met his end a few weeks ago at the hands of a rival gang in Saint Louis.

Within minutes of leaving the city center, he turned off onto a dirt road leading through a thickening forest. The road opened as a field appeared to his left. In the distance, he could see the outline of a weathered farmhouse rising through the trees and brush. Nathaniel slowed as he pulled up to the front of the house and parked beside a well-abused '28 Model A pick-up.

A large shaggy dog bounded up as he turned off the engine. He stepped out of the car and gave the dog a pat on the head before turning his attention to the house where a sturdy line of six young men leaned against the railing of the porch. The slam of a door heralded the arrival of a seventh man, older and more familiar.

"Mr. Chapman." Nathaniel nodded to him.

The farmer stepped down off the porch and held out his hand. "Mr. Blackthorne."

"My apologies for arriving like this." Nathaniel shook his hand. "I needed to speak to you as soon as possible. Is there anywhere we could speak in private?"

Mr. Chapman nodded and gestured toward a barn to the right of the house.

Nathaniel fell into step beside him. He glanced over his shoulder at the boys on the porch. A flicker of movement in the upper story window caught his attention. He saw another figure disappear behind a white lace curtain.

"Quite a family you've got there," he said as they stepped into the barn.

"They're good boys, although, Lord knows I've done the best I can on my own." Mr. Chapman turned toward Nathaniel. "Where's Earl?"

"That's part of the reason I'm here. Earl was killed by a gang of shiners outside of Saint Louis a few weeks back."

Nathaniel shoved his hands in his pockets.

"Damn." Chapman leaned against a large beam next to the hay pile. "His family?"

"They've been well taken care of; you have my word." He cocked his head and pushed away the memory of Earl's wife sobbing as she collapsed to the floor when he'd told her what had happened to her husband. "I always take care of those who are loyal to me."

Mr. Chapman nodded as he stroked his beard. "So, you're here for the shipment details then."

"Until I find a suitable replacement for Earl, yes, I will be finalizing all shipments for transport." He narrowed his gaze. "Unless you feel this changes things."

"I'd be stupid to trust you blindly, Mr. Blackthorne." Chapman eyed him and sighed. "But after nearly ten years of doing business with you...and only you, I'd say we're both in the same boat."

"Shall we continue business then?" Nathaniel smiled. "You do make the best shine on the Mississippi River. Your product has made my establishment one of the most popular in Baton Rouge."

A grin crossed the farmer's lips. "My wife, rest her soul, would have strung me up for gettin' caught up in something like this." He shrugged. "But with seven children and a struggling farm, I had to find a way to keep it all above water."

"Like I said before, I take care of those who are loyal to me. Now, do you have the dozen crates ready for transport?"

"Yes, they're waiting to be loaded. I'll have my two oldest boys deliver them to the dock tonight."

"I will be there to help them unload it." He pulled a small leather bag from his pocket. "Here, with the market the way it is now, silver is a better investment than paper currency." Nathaniel handed the pouch to the awestruck farmer. "That should cover shipments for the next year."

Mr. Chapman opened the bag and peeked inside. He

glanced up at Nathaniel, his eyes wide and jaw trembling. "Thank you for this. When Earl didn't show the other day, I worried...how..." His voice cracked as he took a deep breath. "This will be enough to keep us."

"If you need anything else, contact my associate in Saint Louis, C.R. Evans. He's a lawyer and a close friend of mine. He knows how to contact me in case of an emergency." Nathaniel tipped his hat and turned toward the exit.

A shout echoed from outside before the barn door swung open with a gust of force that nearly knocked Nathaniel onto the ground.

He arched his brow when the wee hellion from the dock barged in, hands on her hips, her long hair fluttering like a cloak around her shoulders.

"Pa, what in the hell is *he* doing here?" she asked, her gaze narrowed on Nathaniel.

"Guard your tongue, Ginny. This is Mr. Blackthorne. He's a business associate."

"Do you often talk business in a barn?" She thrust her jaw out as she directed the question at Nathaniel.

Ignoring her, Nathaniel turned his attention to Mr. Chapman.

"I look forward to working with you. Until tonight." He nodded to the farmer and then walked past the irate young woman whose hazel eyes blazed with irritation.

As Nathaniel stepped out into the yard, the six brothers scattered, barely able to contain their curiosity and amusement at their sister's actions. The young man from earlier at the dock appeared before him.

"I'm sorry, Mr. Blackthorne. Again."

Nathaniel inclined his head and made his way to his car. As the engine roared to life, he noticed Mr. Chapman and Ginny having a heated discussion near the barn. He shook his head. The girl had a fiery spirit and an obvious temper. He did not envy the Chapman men...not one bit.

As he sped down the drive, he caught a glimpse of Ginny

in the rearview mirror watching him.

Ginny seethed as Mr. Blackthorne drove down the dirt road away from the house. She spun around and her brothers scattered, leaving her father standing with his arms crossed, watching her.

"What was that man doing here, Pa?"

"It's none of your business, Virginia."

He stared down at her, concern and frustration etched on his expression.

"But..."

"Stop. Just stop asking questions. It's better if you don't concern yourself with business matters. Now, go inside and make supper. Joshua and Michael will help you clean the fish. David needs to feed the animals." He nodded to her three eldest brothers. "Eric, Matthew, Mark, follow me."

Defeated, Ginny ran toward the house and slammed the front door. She darted to the window in time to see her father and two brothers climb into the pick-up. They drove toward the back of the property right where the fence line disappeared into the forest.

She sighed. *What in the Sam Hill was going on? Who was that man?*

"I brought the fish in, Ginny," Joshua called from the kitchen door.

She vaguely heard her brothers talking in the kitchen. One last glance down the drive showed the dust from the stranger's car had settled. He was the same man from the dock that morning. She'd been completely honest when she said he'd run into her, not the other way around.

He'd spun away from the fish cart so quickly he stepped right into her path. The scent of cedar and pine with a hint of tobacco and spice had caught her off guard. Most people at the dock smelled of fish and river water. He smelled exotic and fresh. His cultured, deep voice with a hint of an English accent only added to it.

His pinstripe suit and perfectly slicked dark hair spoke of money and class. Although, the scruff on his cheeks lent a darker side to such a well-polished man. *Handsome and dangerous, quite a heady combination.* She'd wandered off to find some flour when that braggart stepped into her path. It wasn't as though she'd intentionally run into him. Her heart had pounded when he grabbed ahold of her as though she were no more than a river rat scrounging for coins.

Ginny had never wanted to hit a total stranger as much as she wanted to hit him. The way he handled her so roughly and then treated her with utter disregard. Irritation rose up inside of her.

She stomped into the kitchen to help her brothers filet the fish they'd caught that morning. Joshua and Michael chatted about some of the local girls they'd seen earlier at the market.

Ginny put her knife down and washed her hands. "I'm going out to find some herbs and morels for the fish."

They waved her out the door and resumed their animated conversation. She shook her head. Living with six brothers had taught her one thing: men were simple creatures.

She disappeared into the trees behind the house and made her way to the clearing down by the pond. Many nights she'd slipped down to the pond and gone swimming by moonlight. Sometimes she'd dared to strip completely and let the cool water caress her bare skin.

With no moon the night before, she couldn't venture out for a midnight swim for another few weeks. Soon the summer heat would swelter and spring would be a memory as the humidity made everyone miserable. Then she could swim.

She approached the pond. The memory of the cool water running over her skin made her long for a dip. Pa wouldn't be happy with her leaving the cooking to her brothers, and plain fish for supper again...her stomach heaved at the thought. A bit of mint and morels would brighten the flavor, even if it was catfish. She walked around the pond and farther into the trees.

A barbed wire fence kept the back of the property sectioned off. Her father had forbid her and her brothers to venture past the fence. There were sheer drops where the land had been cut away by an earthquake years ago. Grown over with trees and brush, it made hiking past the fence dangerous. So her father had just put up the fence when they were children to keep them from falling to their deaths.

Ginny walked along the fence searching the ground for any sign of wild mint or morels. She scanned along the big tree bases for the small, sponge-like mushrooms. Late April was the best time to find them. She loved the unique, earthy flavor they possessed.

A small grove beyond the barbed wire fence caught her attention. She spied the mint she needed and a few large, overgrown trees beyond. Surely there were morels hidden in that tiny heaven.

Careful of the barbs, Ginny slipped under the fence and gently picked her way through the brush to where she located tall sprigs of mint. After gathering a few large handfuls of mint leaves and tucking them in her leather bag, she spotted a large oak tree just over the small ridge. Mindful of the treacherous path, she searched the ground as she headed for the tree, the moist dirt squishing beneath her feet.

"There have to be morels here."

A small creek ran just next to the copse of tall oak and sycamore trees. As she rounded the bend, she glanced up to see a building hidden just at the base of the hill, tucked behind the trees, just out of view. *Father never told me there was a building here.* She approached it with caution and peeked into the window.

Copper and glass glinted as the setting sunlight reflected through the holler. She looked around and found a table and glassware as well as sacks of corn stacked against the back wall. The large copper still in the center of the room stole her breath. She'd seen one once...a moonshine still the sheriff had confiscated from one of the local farmers south of Alton.

"What the hell...Pa is making shine?"

Ginny squinted through the glass confirming a distillery set up in the deepest part of the woods behind their small farm. "Pa..."

She slipped into the building and picked up a bottle of shine in a case by the door. Without thinking, she slipped it into her pocket and leaned against the workbench.

A hand clamped down on her shoulder.

"What are you doing here, Ginny?" Her brother, Eric, stood behind her with a stern and angry look on his face. "You know Pa told you to stay out of this part of the woods."

"Is that because he's runnin' shine and doesn't want me to worry?"

She tore herself from his grip, crossing her arms and glaring up at him. Then she realized he wasn't surprised by the building or its contents.

"You knew about this, didn't you?" She lunged at him, pounding her fists against his chest.

"Yes."

A stab of betrayal stung her heart. This time her father and her brothers had pushed her too far. She had believed she was one of the family, that she could be trusted. *Damn them!*

Eric stood there, letting her beat his solid body with her fists. It wouldn't do any good. She glared at him. He took her hand and pulled her into his arms. Ginny didn't want his comfort, or his protection...not anymore. She pushed him away. All the problems, the money, the harassment from the bank, the late nights alone...they all made sense now. Her father and brothers were playing a dangerous game.

She'd heard the stories about the gangs in Saint Louis and Chicago that dealt in shine. Problem was, they didn't like competition. Keeping her distance from Eric, she turned and looked at the still.

"Where's Pa?" she asked with resolve.

"At the house, where you're supposed to be."

"I need to talk to him now." Ginny pushed past him and made her way up the hill.

"Why?" Eric called after her.

Ginny spun around and faced him, her lip trembling. "When I was at Aunt Clara's last week, I saw the prohibition officers asking questions around town. I never thought I'd have to..."

She turned and scrambled up the hill. The thought of her father being arrested or worse, killed by a rival shiner, made her stomach lurch. Once she reached the top of the hill, she ran through the brush, the sound of Eric behind her giving her motivation and a sliver of reassurance.

"Whoa there, Ginny," Eric said, snatching her by the arm. "You cannot tell Pa that you found the still."

"Why the hell not? Did you not hear what I just said?" She jerked her arm away and shoved her hand on her hip.

"I heard you, and I'll tell him about the prohibition officers snooping around town. You cannot, and I repeat, *cannot* tell him you found the still." He stared at her, his eyes intense.

"Why?"

"He'll ship you off."

Her jaw dropped open. "What do you mean he'll ship me off?"

"Pa's been saving up some money to send you back east to stay with Grandma Mable," he replied softly. "This would be the decision maker for him. You know that, right?"

"Why would he ship me off?" she asked, the sadness creeping into her voice.

"Have you seen yourself lately, Gin?" He tugged at her ratty jacket. "Jesus, you look like a boy in that getup. No man's gonna want you looking like a river rat."

Ginny glared at Eric and then glanced down at her

clothes. "Who cares? They're comfortable, and I don't need a man looking at me."

He reached out and tipped her chin up, forcing her to meet his eyes. "I know, but you have to plan for your future. You can't live on this farm your whole life. You need to get cleaned up. Get married, have some kids. Make a life for yourself." He gestured back to the hollow where the distillery hid. "This is no life for a lady."

"But I'm your sister," she whispered, her heart breaking at the thought of leaving the only life she'd ever known. Of having to change into something other than who she knew she was.

"All the more reason for you to go." Eric brushed his thumb along her cheek. "You're nearly twenty, Gin. It's time for you to move on with your life."

She pushed his hand away and made her way toward the house. When she reached the barbed wire fence, she shoved herself through, tearing her jacket and scratching her arm. It stung, but not unlike the thought of leaving her family.

As she approached the house, Ginny noticed an unfamiliar red Ford in the drive. The sleek lines screamed Roadster. The sound of shouting from the front of the house made her stop.

Eric pulled her by the arm until they were both hidden by the large oak tree beyond the house. The shouting continued, followed by some breaking glass. Ginny buried her head against her brother's chest.

"Who are they?" she whispered. "What do they want?"

"Shhh, I don't know."

All her life, Ginny had been lied to, coddled, even though they treated her like one of the boys most of the time. Betrayal and fear had shot through her at the sight of her father's distillery. The bottle in her pocket sank like a stone against her leg, weighing her down.

"Get off my land!"

Her father's booming voice made her tremble. Eric

tightened his grip on her and brought his lips to her ear. "Listen carefully, Ginny. You remember all those times Pa made you take the path through the forest into town?"

She nodded, licking her lips. What was he saying?

"If anything happens, take that path. Stay off the main roads. Go straight to Aunt Clara's house. Don't stop for anything or anyone, you hear me?" His grip tightened on her arms, pinching her skin.

She pulled back to look at his face. The fear in his eyes terrified her.

"Eric, what are you talking about? Why?"

"No questions, not now."

A gunshot echoed through the clearing.

Eric's gaze, wide with fear, drifted toward the house.

"Go, Ginny. Run and don't look back." He hugged her tight. "I will find you."

He kissed her forehead and pushed her toward the woods.

Ginny darted into the trees, clutching her jacket close, shielding her face from the gnarly branches as they grabbed at the rough fabric. She tripped over a stone, stumbling briefly, but picked up speed as she located the small deer path that led toward town.

Several gunshots echoed behind her. She dashed the tears away with the back of her hand. Part of her wanted to look back...to go back...but the expression on her brother's face had said it all. Her family was in trouble. She'd always known her brothers and father were overprotective, but it was only now she realized why.

Eric vowed he would find her. She'd never known him not to keep a promise. The sun had set by the time she reached town. Turning down the alley, she noticed the same red Ford Roadster parked on the street in front of her aunt's townhome. Fear infused her.

"Where do I go now?"

On instinct, she wove her way toward the river...toward

the docks. When she reached them, her gaze lighted over the ships there.

A familiar figure stood near the steamer ship, the Mississippi Queen. It was that shady bloke from earlier — Mr. Blackthorne. He had to know something. She moved to approach him, when the red Roadster pulled up to the dock. Two men in fedoras, one in a black and white pinstripe suit and the other in a dark brown duster, stepped out and approached Blackthorne.

Ginny's heart raced. Was he part of their gang? *What should I do?* She closed her eyes and spied several crates to still be loaded and an oversized steamer trunk. Her gaze flittered to the three men. The two men began to argue with Mr. Blackthorne.

Nodding to herself, Ginny opened the steamer trunk and pulled all the clothes out, tossing them in the river behind her. For once, being so petite had an advantage. She pulled the trunk closed as best she could, leaving a small crack by which to breathe, and waited.

Her last image was of the Englishman turning toward her as the lid snapped closed.

CHAPTER TWO

Ginny's heart stopped. If she screamed, they would find her. She bit her tongue to keep from shouting. Panic consumed her as the trunk began to rock and sway as someone lifted and began to carry it.

"Damned heavy, what in the hell is he packing in here?" A muffled voice sounded from the outside of the trunk.

"We're not paid to ask questions," a second man replied. "C'mon let's get these trunks loaded. The ship sails in a few minutes."

The rocking of the small confined space nearly made Ginny pass out. She shouldn't have hidden in his trunk. It was a stupid, impulsive thing to do, but the memory of the men in the Roadster, seeing them argue with Blackthorne, made her fear the worst about her family's fate. She shivered. *What would happen if they found me?*

The trunk hit the floor with a thud, jarring her deep to her bones and rattling her teeth. She lay there in the dark until she heard their footsteps recede and the door close. *I need to get out of here before Blackthorne comes.* After pushing her weight against the lid, she froze at the realization of her predicament. *I'm locked inside this trunk.*

Ginny kicked at the lid. Wedging her foot up against the top didn't give her a whole lot of room to work. The space constricted while the darkness disoriented her. Her breath came in short pants and spots began to float before her eyes. She'd been scared before, but a sudden rush of terror threatened to pull her beneath the waves of fear.

What if he finds me? What if he returns me to those men? Ginny panicked, beating on the trunk lid with her fists, feeling the flakes of paper fall on her face as she scratched at the inside of her little coffin. She refused to scream, but a soft whimper escaped her lips as the tears pooled at the corner of her eyes.

Her father was right. *I am trouble. This is penance for my wicked behavior.* Locked in a strange man's trunk, bound for New Orleans or God knew where on a shady, average-sized riverboat. Yes, the good Lord was demanding penance for her childish behavior.

She kicked the lid one last time, then settled on the few articles of clothing remaining in the trunk, folding her arms across her chest. Ginny let the tears fall.

A door opened. She heard the creaking of the hinges, the sound of footsteps on the floorboards right beside the trunk.

Ginny stilled and held her breath. A soft hiccup escaped her.

The lock rattled against the trunk. *He's opening it.*

She closed her eyes, willing herself a thousand miles away. When the light hit her face, she nearly sighed with relief.

"You could have just asked to come along instead of caging yourself in my trunk." He smiled down at her, the harsh lines of his stern expression softening a bit at the action.

As she slowly climbed from her tomb, she paused to brush off her pants and tuck her hair back under her cap.

"I'd hoped to be gone before you returned to your cabin." She moved toward the door. "I'll go."

He reached out and caught her wrist. "Why were you hiding in my luggage?"

Ginny bit her tongue, knowing her life was already in danger and unsure as to his role in what transpired at her farm earlier that evening. "I was running away."

"Life at home that rough for you? Don't you have an army of brothers to protect you?"

"Not when they can't even protect themselves," she murmured under her breath.

"Did something happen after I left your farm?" His eyes darkened with concern and interest.

"I went to gather herbs in the woods, and when I came back..." She hesitated.

"You don't trust me." He offered a lopsided smirk. "I don't blame you." His expression turned serious. "But if your family is in some kind of danger, I may be able to help."

Ginny shook her head. "It's too late."

His grip tightened on her wrist as he pulled her closer and tipped her chin up with his other hand.

"What happened?"

"I came back and my father was arguing with two men. Then I heard gun shots. I ran." She didn't volunteer any other details.

"Did you see what they were driving?" His tone turned cold.

"Yeah, they were driving a red hotrod."

She shook her head and dropped her gaze. The tears pooled in the corner of her eyes. *Is my family...dead?* She couldn't bring herself to speak the words. Her body shook with rage and grief.

He sat down on the edge of the cabin bed and pulled her against him, wrapping her in a comforting embrace. His hands strong and his body warm. The scent of him soothing and strangely familiar.

He froze as his hand rested on her hip, then slipped it into her pocket and withdrew her only link to home. The bottle of moonshine.

"That's some pretty expensive booze you got there, kid. Have you been keeping secrets from me?" He met her gaze, his expression suddenly unreadable as he searched her face.

The heat rushed to her cheeks. Ginny pulled away from him, grabbing her bottle from his hand and putting it back in her pocket.

"I'm leaving."

"Where do you plan on going? We've already left the dock if you haven't noticed."

She turned to face him again, noting the amused smile playing on his lips. "You can't keep me prisoner here."

"If you leave this room, they will catch onto your scent faster than a hound on a fox." He cocked his head. "Vixen to be precise."

Ginny glanced down at her clothes — the ones he'd called rags earlier that day — wondering why he'd call her such a thing. It wasn't like she even looked like a woman in her brother's hand-me-down clothes.

"What happened here?" he asked reaching for her arm.

She jerked out of his grasp, keeping him in her sights. "What?"

"Your arm," he said, gesturing to her torn sleeve. "Take your jacket off."

Shaking her head, she backed away. "What are you going to do?"

He grasped her arm and pulled her back to sit beside him on the bed. She tried to escape him again, but his grip tightened on her arms.

"Listen to me, kid. I promise to help you if you'll quit resisting me."

Ginny stilled. "I still don't trust you."

"I'm not asking you to trust me." He sighed. "Your father worked for me for years. I promised I would care for those who were loyal to me."

"Loyalty doesn't ensure trust," she mumbled.

"True, but I can't toss you into the river or feed you to the wolves by allowing you to leave this room." Gently, he peeled the jacket from her shoulders. "Until I can return you to your family, you will be under my care."

She winced as the fabric brushed against her arm. "I'm not a child."

His gaze drifted down across her chest and then drifted

to the wound on her arm.

"I can see that." He cleared his throat. "How old are you?"

"I will be twenty in December."

Their eyes met and the light illuminated his face perfectly surprise and disbelief mingled in his mismatched eyes. This time she noticed the subtle difference in their color. *One blue and one green.*

"I wouldn't have put you a day over fourteen."

"Many people mistake me not only for a boy, but a child." She grinned. "Such assumptions can prove advantageous."

"You sound educated as well." He glanced at her as he shifted the torn fabric of her sleeve away from the cut on her right arm.

"I attended Miss Brook's Finishing School for Girls in Saint Louis. My aunt's gift to my father."

She looked at the far wall of the cabin and winced as he turned her arm. "As you can see, it did nothing to make me a lady."

"And your mother?" he asked. "Where is she?"

"She died giving birth when I was five."

He nodded. "Give me the moonshine."

Her gaze snapped to his. "Why?"

"I want to disinfect this wound. That bottle is your saving grace." He reached in her pocket and withdrew the shine. She watched helpless as he uncorked it and poured a little on a handkerchief he'd pulled from his vest. He dabbed a bit on the cloth and pressed it liberally to the wound.

A sharp stinging sensation shot up her arm as he cleaned it.

"Ouch!" She jumped and tried to pull away, but he held her steady.

"Are you sure you're not a child? You certainly act like one." He held her arm up and blew across the alcohol-dampened wound.

Ginny whimpered. His hot breath against her skin eased the discomfort, but it also unleashed a curious churning need somewhere deep inside her. She swayed against him.

"You should get some rest." He released her arm and stood. "You can sleep here. I'll go find you some suitable clothing." He motioned to the bed and then glanced at the open trunk. "I see I shall have to find some clothing for myself as well."

She felt her cheeks heat but couldn't bring herself to apologize to him for throwing his clothing in the river. Her body still thrummed from his ministrations.

"Is there anything else you require, kid?" he asked as he picked up the moonshine and tucked it into his own pocket.

"Virginia."

He glanced at her. "Pardon?"

"My name is Virginia...most people call me Ginny."

"Well then, Virginia. I shall return momentarily." He gave her a pointed look. "Do not leave this cabin."

She nodded, and he slipped out the door. Ginny collapsed back against the bed and stared at the ceiling. The events of the day crept upon her like a mudslide. Her brother's vow echoed in the back of her mind.

"Eric, please be alive."

Nathaniel leaned against the wall next to the door. Inside, he could hear Virginia's soft sobs. *Damn.* He pushed off in search of Levi. As he wandered toward the captain's quarters, he raked his hand through his hair. *What in the hell happened to her family? Why does she look so terrified?*

The thought of her being afraid of him should have brought him comfort, but it did not. That morning on the docks, he saw her defiant spirit...the survivor deep within her. But when he'd opened his trunk and found her, she looked as though she'd shatter with a single touch.

She didn't trust him, which was obvious. Not that he could blame her. He obviously owed her an explanation about his involvement with her father. There had to be a reason why she would have run away from the safety of her family and stowed away in his luggage. Hadn't she mentioned an aunt? Why did she not seek asylum there? There were far too many questions and not nearly enough answers.

His thoughts turned to the Garrett brothers who had approached him near the dock. The gaudy Ford Roadster they drove gave them away. Although he tried to play it off as disinterest on his part, their questions had set him on edge. Now he knew why. They'd been honing in on his territory, testing him. And that placed Virginia's family square in their sights.

Nathaniel wandered down the hall until he reached the captain's door. He knocked.

"Come in."

He pushed open the door and stepped into the room, carefully closing the door behind him. The room wasn't much bigger than his own quarters and sported a large bed with a writing desk and a small area for luggage. Simple and clean, the style he'd come to expect from Levi over the years.

"My apologies for the intrusion, Levi. But I have a bit of a problem."

Levi glanced up from the papers he had on his desk. He turned to face Nathaniel and frowned. "What sort of problem?"

"It seems as though I picked up a stowaway in my luggage." He held his hand up. "That's not the problem. She's the daughter of my supplier. I'm not sure why she's here, but I fear something has happened to her family."

"Would you like me to send one of the men back on foot to do some digging?" Levi asked, his expression serious.

"If you wouldn't mind. I'd like to have more information

before I ship her back home, for her own safety."

"I'll ask Jim to go right away and have him relay any information to your place in Baton Rouge. We should have answers by the time we reach port there."

"I believe the Garrett brothers had something to do with it." Nathaniel folded his arms across his chest. "Have them keep an eye on those bastards as well."

"The Garretts?" Levi's gaze snapped to his, narrowing slightly as he reached for his pipe. "What makes you say that?"

"That damned Roadster Ned hotrods around town. Virginia saw it at her farm before they started shooting."

"Jesus Christ," Levi swore as he tossed the pipe onto his desk. "I'll have Jim check it all out."

"I appreciate it. Also, if you have some extra clothing, it seems as though mine has disappeared. I'll also need some fresh clothes for the girl. A pair of trousers and a shirt or two should do well enough." Nathaniel nodded before he turned to leave. "I've instructed her to stay in the cabin until we reach our destination."

"I'd offer you another cabin, but unfortunately we are fully manned at the moment with no available bunks." Levi picked up a stack of books in the corner of the room and handed them to Nathaniel. "These will keep her occupied until we dock. How old is she?"

"Old enough to cause trouble," Nathaniel said as he opened the door. He heard Levi's soft chuckle as he latched it behind him.

Levi's man would get answers, then they could make a decision concerning her fate once they reached Baton Rouge. No sense in worrying about what he couldn't address. Perhaps the time they had together would bring her to trust him.

As he walked down the corridor, he heard the faint strains of singing coming from his cabin. He paused just outside the door and leaned his ear against it. A voice sweet as honeysuckle and yet as sinful as shine drifted through the wood. He listened, letting her soft melody soothe him, caress him, seduce him.

He remembered the look on her face, the tremble of her body as he blew against her wound. He'd only meant to dry the area, but it ignited something inside of him. Something carnal and dangerous. Something he hadn't allowed himself to feel since he'd left England...since Sarah. He shook his head.

I'll not let that happen again. Nathaniel pushed open the door and the intoxicating music ceased instantly.

Ginny stood, her hair a mass of tangled waves hanging down to her waist. She saw the books in his arms and her expression blossomed with joy.

"Are these for me?" she asked, snatching the books from his arms.

A pang of pleasure struck deep in his chest. He'd forgotten how good it felt to bring such an innocent feeling of joy to someone. "Presumptuous little river rat, aren't you?" He sighed, trying to hide his amusement to her reaction. "Yes, they're for you."

"*Pride and Prejudice, Frankenstein*, ohhhhh, is this *Huckleberry Finn*?" Her eyes glittered in the lamplight.

He wanted to steal some of her delight for himself.

A soft knock at the door broke his thoughts. He answered it to find a pile of blankets and some clothes sitting outside. Levi could always be counted on to come through in a pinch. He hefted the pile of fabric and took it inside, dropping it on the bed next to Virginia who sat engrossed in one of the novels.

He shook his head and latched the door. Grabbing one of the blankets, he quickly affixed it between the corner of the boarded window and a small hook near the door. It conveniently corded off a section of the cabin to provide privacy should one need to change or...well, other reasons.

Nathaniel turned to Virginia. "You should get some

sleep." He plucked the book from her hands and took it as well as the rest and set them in his trunk. "There will be plenty of time for you to read on the trip."

"Where are we going?" she asked, excitement lacing her voice.

"Baton Rouge." He placed a blanket on her bed, afraid to look at her and lose himself.

"How long will it take us?" She picked through the clothing laying on his bed and selected an oversized cream-colored shirt and a pair of trousers.

"Just under a week."

Virginia frowned and clutched the clothes against her chest. "I have to stay locked up in this room for a week!"

He watched her from the corner of his eye. "Yes. I've brought you plenty of things to read. If you need something else to occupy your mind, I will see what I can find. But you must not leave this cabin under any circumstances." Nathaniel turned to face her. "Is that understood?"

"I've lived on the river my entire life. Not to mention having to live with my father and six brothers." Ginny scoffed. "Nothing on this boat could possibly shock me."

She smirked, defiant and confident, but he saw the hint of uncertainty in her hazel eyes.

Nathaniel stepped closer, and she backed away from him as he invaded her space. When her back slammed against the wall, he caged her in, his hands resting beside her head.

She dropped the clothes and pressed her balled fists against his chest. "What are you doing?"

"If they find out you're on this ship, you will be putting yourself in danger. I cannot be your chaperone for the duration of this trip, so leaving this room is forbidden. Do you understand what would happen if they found you wandering the ship alone?" He narrowed his gaze and frowned.

The defiance turned to terrified realization.

"Not all the men on this ship are loyal to me, most are just here for the money. I cannot be assured what their intentions are toward a young, attractive woman. If they find a treasure like you aboard, I doubt they'll leave you untouched." Nathaniel tried not to think of the implication of his warning.

Ginny's lips parted on a gasp as he leaned close. His body pressed against hers.

"Tell me, river rat. Are you still a virgin?"

Her cheeks flared red. "What does that matter?"

"Because if you are, then I intend to take extra care of you until I can return you to your father. In the exact condition I found you." He arched his brow when her anger melted into something akin to shock. The air around them pulsed with a strange energy. Nathaniel took a few steps back, releasing her.

"Was that necessary?" she asked, moving to pick up the clothing.

"Are you going to heed my advice and remain here for the length of the trip?" He refused to even look at her, but instead focused on the lantern hanging in the corner of the room. His body rioted against good sense. Being so near her, seeing her react to him in such a way, made him want much more than he should even consider. Perhaps he was as much of a threat to her as the scoundrels Levi employed.

"Yes." She tossed the clothing to the bed.

"Good girl." He stalked toward the door.

"Thank you."

Her voice echoed behind him, a mixture of sweet torment and innocence. It took all his effort not to release the desire he knew raged just below the surface. A desire he'd restrained for years. He nodded and left the cabin, shutting the door firmly behind him.

CHAPTER THREE

Dumbstruck, Ginny watched the door close behind him.

"I try to thank him for coming to my aid, he ignores me. I threaten to defy him, he pins me against the wall as if he's about to ravish me." She pressed her hand to her racing heart. On a whim, she stuck her tongue out at the door. "Insufferable man."

Her attention focused on the pile of clothes on the bed. At least she had her own space, for now.

With a heavy sigh, Ginny eyed the basin of water and a rag. She stripped off the dirty clothing and used a rag to clean the grime from her body before putting the fresh clothing on.

Feeling refreshed, Ginny wandered to the trunk where he'd placed the books. She selected one of them at random and climbed into the bed. Settling beneath the blanket, she sighed.

"What have I gotten myself into?" she asked herself under her breath. Ginny pushed away all the events of the day and focused on the book in her hands. *Frankenstein.*

Boarding school had afforded her an education, a chance at becoming a proper lady, but it never allowed her to read anything for her own amusement. The classics, Shakespeare and Chaucer, were so dry. She opened the book and soon became absorbed by the story between the pages.

Several chapters later, a soft knock distracted her from the riveting tale. Reluctantly, she set the book aside and stared at the door, unsure if she should answer or wait for the person on the other side to come in.

"Yes?" she asked in a horrible attempt to disguise her voice as a man's. She cringed at her own idiocy. Her ability to hide her sex in men's clothes obviously did nothing to quell the feminine lilt of her voice.

The door swung open revealing a square-shouldered, bearded man wearing a well-worn navy blue cap. His long, straight hair was pulled back and tied at the nape of his neck with a faded ribbon. He entered the room and closed the door behind him as his gaze swept over the room. When he spotted her on the bunk, he smiled.

"Hello there, stowaway."

She damn near fainted. His grin oozed charm, his voice smooth as the velvet damask her aunt coveted at the Sears and Roebuck. While Ginny considered herself immune to handsome men, this man could have asked her to jump in the river and swim to Baton Rouge...and she would have if only to hear him speak to her again.

"Stowaway?" she squeaked.

He approached her and pulled something from his pocket. A bag of lemon drop candies.

Ginny licked her lips absently as he set them on the bed. She met his gaze, the depths of his brown eyes mesmerized her. Then she realized...they'd discovered she was on board. Fear replaced all other thoughts in her mind.

"Don't panic," he said, leaning against the wall. "I promise, no one will find you. Well, besides Nathaniel and me."

"Who are you?" She snatched the bag and popped a candy in her mouth. The tart lemon mixed with the sugar on her tongue. Ginny whimpered with pure delight.

He cleared his throat and averted his gaze.

Heat rose in her cheeks again. *I've never blushed so much in my entire life.* Ginny tucked the remainder of the bag under her pillow.

When he finally looked at her again, he grinned. "I'm the

captain. You can call me Levi."

"*You're* the captain?" Ginny wanted to hide under the blankets and never come out.

"I am." Levi tipped his cap back. His bearded jaw and straight white teeth were at odds with each other, yet it suited him. His blue eyes sparkled with humor.

Everything about him suited her. He reminded her of her brothers, and yet his handsome face made her stomach twist in knots at his scrutiny as he studied her. He didn't make her heart pound like Blackthorne, but he seemed more open and lighthearted. Much like her brother, Eric.

Ginny shook the thoughts from her mind.

He nodded to the book on her lap. "I see you're enjoying the books."

"I am." Ginny beamed and nodded to the books sitting in the open trunk. "Are they yours?"

"They are. I keep them on board for the long trips, but since you're confined to this room, I figured you could use them more than me."

"Thank you." She held the worn copy of *Frankenstein* against her chest.

He pushed away from the wall and backed toward the door. "Should you need anything, please let me know." Levi winked and added, "If you tire of Nathaniel, I wouldn't mind keeping you company."

He laughed as he stepped out into the hallway and closed the door behind him.

"Nathaniel?" Ginny pondered to the empty cabin. A familiar image of Blackthorne popped into her mind. "Nathaniel Blackthorne." She chuckled. "It sounds like a proper British name too."

Ginny heard the sound of raised voices in the hallway. Before she could get out of bed, he strolled in as if pulled from her thoughts, his hair mussed and blood on his lip.

"Nathaniel, what happened?" She rushed to his side.

He glanced at her in surprise and then scowled.

"Nothing."

"Sit down on the bed," Ginny ordered.

The man stood well over a foot taller than her. He hesitated for a moment before collapsing on the bed. She pulled a handkerchief from the trunk and dug to the bottom to locate the bottle of moonshine hidden next to the books.

Ginny dabbed a bit of the shine on the cloth and stood before the brooding Brit. "Look up."

He raised his chin and their eyes locked. A trickle of blood smeared across his mouth when he pressed his full lips together.

"Stop scowling." She grasped his chin in her hand. "Open your mouth."

When he parted his lips, Ginny sighed and wiped the blood away, finally locating the split on his lower lip. She rubbed the alcohol on it, and he winced at the sting. The familiar pain echoed from his ministration on her arm earlier.

Without thinking, she leaned close and blew across his swollen, split lip.

Her gaze drifted up, noting the way his nostrils flared, the way the color of his eyes became consumed by the dark centers. She blew again, and he pinched his eyes closed. The split would heal, but she couldn't halt the sudden desire to press a kiss to the cut. A childish effort to make it better clouded by a darker, more carnal desire.

A hint of disappointment settled in her stomach when he put his hands on her shoulders and pushed her back.

"What happened?" she asked, turning away from him and pressing her hand to her stomach.

"I see Levi decided to introduce himself." He sounded almost bitter.

Ginny spun around. "Did you two fight?"

He grunted. "A friendly disagreement."

"Over me?" She couldn't help but grin.

Nathaniel scoffed. "Don't be ridiculous. I'm merely trying to keep you safe...from everyone on this ship, until I can return you to your family." He pointed a finger at her. "Don't trust him."

"I'm not a child," she reminded him. "I don't need you to cluck at me constantly like a mother hen."

He scowled at her.

"Besides, if you don't trust him, why did you tell him I was here?"

"I trust him with my goods, with my ship, with everything else...but not with you." He stood and raked a hand through his hair.

"Why not?" Ginny licked her lips and imagined running her hands through his hair. She'd only ever seen it slicked back and parted perfectly, but when he mussed it with his hand, it laid across his forehead in tumultuous waves. He looked so handsome all ruffled and distraught.

"Because we're not good men, Virginia."

"We? Are you including yourself in that group?" She clenched her fists tight to keep from reaching for him. Her words were a misguided attempt to understand him, and yet against all the danger and uncertainty, she longed to know who he was beneath it all.

"Yes." He pointed to the bed. "You should get some sleep."

"Again, I'm not a child, Nathaniel. Stop treating me like one." She saw the muscle twitch in his jaw as the wheels turned in his mind.

"Fine." He sat down on the opposite side of the bed, kicked off his shoes, and lay down. Not even bothering to pull the blanket over his body, he turned his back to her to face the wall.

Irritated and exhausted by the onslaught of emotions, Ginny climbed under the blankets. She reached out and drew the lantern close, extinguishing it with one blow. As her eyes adjusted to the darkness, she sank onto the bed and pulled the blanket over herself, tucking it beneath her chin.

The events of the last day settled on her heavy heart.

Between Nathaniel and Levi, the men who'd attacked her family, and the dangerous reality of her situation, Ginny found herself lost on the river and exhausted from her mind running in circles.

I miss them. I hope they're alive. Silent tears spilled across her checks. Ginny closed her eyes and willed the pain to cease its relentless ache. Handsome and kind as Nathaniel was, his arrival in her life had caused her nothing but pain.

Thoughts of her family plagued her as the darkness and the motion of the ship lulled her to sleep. *I wish I were home. I wish I'd never met Nathaniel Blackthorne.*

A scream shattered the silence of the cabin. Nathaniel nearly tumbled from the bed.

Virginia thrashed beside him. He reached out and pulled her toward him for fear she would fall to the floor. He cradled her against his chest.

Her body trembled, but she never opened her eyes. Whimpers escaped from her pursed lips. He held her close as he rocked her. After he crawled beneath the blankets, he held her tight against him until what remained of the nightmares had faded.

His heart calmed when he saw her expression relax and she nuzzled closer to his warmth. *Lord, have mercy.*

Nathaniel had struggled for hours to fall asleep thanks to his altercation with Levi and the subsequent conversation with Virginia. When she'd pursed her lips and her lemon scented breath caressed his skin, he'd nearly hauled her into his lap and kissed her senseless.

Pushing her away had been the only way for him to recover some of his sanity. He glanced down at the woman in his arms. "What am I going to do with you, kid?"

Set her free, echoed in the back of his mind. He sighed and stroked a strand of hair from her face.

When he was sure restful sleep had finally descended on her, Nathaniel laid her on the center of the bed, tucked the blankets around her tiny frame, and quickly pulled on his shoes. Stepping out into the hall, he heard commotion on the deck. After making sure the door was firmly shut behind him, he made his way to the wheelhouse.

The crew stood huddled on the main deck shrouded in morning twilight. A sapphire hue mixed with the burgeoning sunrise over the treetops. Nathaniel joined them.

"What's going on here?" he asked.

The men turned toward him, their expressions full of fear and uncertainty.

"We heard her," one of the men said, his gaze darting out over the river.

"Who?" Nathaniel crossed his arms. Had they somehow discovered Virginia's presence on the ship?

"The Drowned Woman."

A wave of relief washed over Nathaniel. They didn't know about Virginia. He glanced at Levi, who stood leaning against the railing. Their eyes met in a silent agreement. With a nod, Levi turned his attention back to them.

"There's no reason to worry, men. There's never been a confirmed sighting of her." Levi pulled out his pipe and lit it. He put on an air of confidence in an attempt to allay their superstitious fears.

"Legend has it she pulls men overboard and drowns them. She seeks revenge, looking for the man who killed her," one of the men added, his hand shaking as he reached for a cigarette in his pocket.

Nathaniel vaguely remembered the story. Seeing the men react in such a manner would have been amusing had it not been for the thick tension in the air, creeping, cloistering, constricting. For him it lay like a loadstone around his neck...all because of that slip of a girl.

A strangled laugh escaped him.

"Nervous nellies, the lot of you. The spirits want nothing to do with us. Remember, fear the living, not the dead." He swept his arm toward the sunrise as it began its ascension over the horizon. "Back to work."

The men dispersed leaving Levi and Nathaniel standing near the port railing. Levi turned to stare out over the water.

"You should be more careful with her," Levi murmured.

"She had a nightmare...screamed in her sleep." Nathaniel folded his arms across his chest.

The captain's head snapped up. "Is she okay?"

A hint of irritation nagged at the back of Nathaniel's conscience. "She'll be fine. Never even woke up."

"What happened to her? What brought her to this point?" Levi asked.

"The girl had no idea of her father's alternate profession. She found out somehow and claims when she returned to the house to confront him, there were two men already there doing just that." He ran his hand across his jaw. "Gunfire chased her into the woods. She ran into town and stowed away in my trunk."

"Why you?"

Nathaniel frowned and shrugged. "I haven't figured that out yet. I can tell she's holding back, keeping things from me."

Levi chuckled. "Can't say as I blame her for that, considering the circumstances."

"She ran into me on the docks yesterday, right before I met with you." Nathaniel leaned his elbows on the railing and looked out over the river, listening to the rhythmic churning of the paddle wheel. "I thought she was a boy, dressed in those rags with her hair tucked into a cap. Then I go to meet with Mr. Chapman and discover the pretty river rat is the daughter of my supplier." He shook his head.

"Fate has her designs set on you it seems." Levi offered a sympathetic smile. "She doesn't seem much older than fifteen."

"She'll be twenty in December, or so she tells me."

Nathaniel glared at his friend. "Don't make me give you a matching pair." He pointed to Levi's bruised cheekbone. "The girl is off limits."

"Is that because you've already claimed her?"

"Until I return to Alton, she's under my protection. I can't shake the feeling that she's in this mess because of me." He turned to Levi. "Once I get information from the man you sent back to Alton, I'll know for sure."

"You thinking one of the gangs caught wind of your supplier?" Levi straightened, his expression somber.

"The Garrett brothers have been sniffing around my operation for years so I've been careful to distance myself from my supplier. But I'm almost positive they're responsible for Earl's death."

"There are a half a dozen gangs in Saint Louis that would love to get their hands on your shine supplier. What makes you so sure it's not one of them?"

Nathaniel leveled his gaze with Levi. "Because they stopped to have a chat before we left last evening."

"That red Ford Roadster?" Levi let out a low whistle. "Not exactly keeping their nose to the ground, but I can't fault their taste. It was classy."

"My Lincoln has class; that coupe is garish. It'll draw far too much attention to them if they're not careful."

"What are you going to do once you reach Baton Rouge?"

Nathaniel pondered for a moment and then replied, "I'll wait for your man to send me information. I need to find out what happened at that farm. Once I get more details, I'll contact my lawyer and have him do some legwork."

"Why don't you just drop the shipment and then take her back?"

"I need to be sure I'm not returning her to a hornet's nest. If they found my supplier, she's no longer safe there." Nathaniel smoothed his hand over his hair. No matter how clear the waters seemed, he needed to test their depth before diving headfirst.

"What are you going to do with her in Baton Rouge?" Levi smirked. "I can keep her with me on the ship."

Nathaniel nearly growled at his friend's teasing offer. "She'll stay with me."

Levi raised his hands in a show of surrender.

"So you plan on what, hiding her in the back room of your club? It's not like you can have a girl who barely looks fifteen wandering around a place with a reputation such as yours." He narrowed his gaze meaningfully. "You're just asking for trouble."

"Damn it." Nathaniel sighed. "I may have to take her to Pamela."

"Whoa there. Pamela's place is a whole other level of dangerous, especially for her. She'd be safer at the club."

"I mean, Pamela can help me hide her."

"By what, stuffing her in a corset and auctioning her off to the highest bidder?" Levi shook his head. "You'll be throwing her to the wolves."

Nathaniel wanted to throw something at his dim-witted friend. "Pamela can help me transform her into a lady. I've seen what that woman can do with makeup and several yards of silk."

"What are you saying?"

"Pamela can help me disguise her. No one will know she's a little river rat from Alton, and better yet, I can keep her with me. Hide her in plain sight. No one will ever piece the two together."

Levi scoffed. "If you or Pamela can turn her into a lady, I'll eat my hat. She's cute and she's got potential, but a lady...you might be putting all your eggs in a rotting basket."

"We've been friends for a long time, Levi. Don't make me throw you into the river with concrete blocks strapped to your ankles."

"Hah, I'd like to see you try. Besides, I'm the only one you trust to run booze for you."

"You overestimate my tolerance for you." Nathaniel grinned. "Speaking of the next run. I'll need you to take *The Sentinel* to New Orleans to pick up the next shipment. You'll take a case of the shine with you to trade for the rum." He narrowed his gaze at his friend. "Stay away from the gaming dens in New Orleans. I won't bail your ass out again, Levi."

"Shall I leave the rest of the cargo on the *Mississippi Queen* until they're both in the dock?" Levi tapped the ashes from his pipe and stuffed new tobacco in it, blatantly ignoring Nathaniel's warning.

"Yes, I'll have James and Victor stand watch while you make the short trip to New Orleans."

At Levi's nod, the two fell into a companionable silence.

"I'm serious you know." Nathaniel turned to Levi. "I won't always be around to save you from your addiction."

"I'm not addicted to it." Levi took a puff from his pipe. "It's just a harmless hobby."

"Harmless? You nearly lost your hand the last time you couldn't pay your debts with that foreign dignitary when he claimed you'd cheated." Nathaniel shook his head. "You're playing with fire."

Levi sighed. "No more than you are."

The truth hung between them in the still morning air. The sunlight shone through the treetops reflecting on the water, its warmth already dismissing the chill of the early morning hours. The rushing of the water through the wheel played a rhythmic beat to the birdsong melody echoing from the riverbank.

Levi lit his pipe and tossed the match into the water. "Do you want to take my cabin?"

Nathaniel glanced up, startled by the offer. "So you can have an excuse to check on her? I don't think so."

He shook his head. "That's not what I meant. It's obvious you're not going to get much sleep in that cabin. Use mine if you need your own space." A smirk crossed Levi's lips before he tucked the pipe between his teeth.

"I don't want to leave her alone for too long." Nathaniel ran his hand through his hair, mussing it completely. He sighed. "Thanks."

"You know where to find me." Levi clapped his hand on Nathaniel's shoulder as he passed and disappeared into the stairwell leading up to the wheelhouse.

Nathaniel hung his head. The routine trip proved to be much more complicated than he'd anticipated. His supplier had been attacked and he'd inherited a girl who teased him to the point where he wanted to ruin her, damn the consequences. His body ached at the memory of her careful, tender touch when she treated his injuries.

What the hell am I going to do with that river rat?

CHAPTER FOUR

Five days. Ginny fumed as she threw the book across the room. She'd read every book Levi had given her. Twice. But that wasn't the worst part. Nathaniel had been absent for every one of those days. He didn't come to the cabin, not to sleep, not to check on her, nothing. He'd completely abandoned her to her own devices.

And that pissed her off.

Part of her wondered why he suddenly shunned her. His teasing moments. The kindness he'd shown her. They disintegrated like paper in the water. She'd woken up to an empty room that first day, and he'd never returned after that.

Levi had brought her food and water. He sat and talked with her a few times in an attempt to pass some time and make her smile. But as charming as the captain was, her heart ached at the solitude and Nathaniel's absence. It infuriated her how he could isolate her from the world and then abandon her as well.

She flopped down on the bed. The sound of the paddle's rhythm against the water and the boiler transformed into a soothing comfort over the last few days, but at the same time it had become almost hypnotic to the point of madness.

"I need to get out of this room, just for an hour," she murmured. The only window in the room had been locked and boarded. Slivers of light shown through the cracks, but Ginny craved the kiss of the sun on her face, the gentle touch of the wind on her skin.

She slipped off the bed and tried the door again. *Locked.*

"I hate you, Nathaniel Blackthorne," she whispered to the door, praying he somehow heard her. The wicked part of her wanted to shout it, scream it so they heard it on the riverbanks.

The sound of approaching footsteps caught her by surprise. Ginny backed away from the door just as the lock clicked. Levi stood in the doorway with a plate in his hand.

"I thought you might be hungry." He closed the door behind him.

Ginny flopped onto the bed again, burying her face in the pillow and screaming.

"Something wrong?" Levi asked, once she finished her tantrum.

"I. Can't. Stay. In this room. One. More. Second." Her words were clipped, marking every ounce of her irritation.

He set the plate down and sat beside her on the bed.

"We'll be arriving the next day or two. The second boiler is giving me problems, otherwise we would have been there tonight."

Ginny frowned. "Is that supposed to make me feel better?"

He shrugged. "Sorry, I thought maybe if you had an end in sight, it would make the trip easier. It won't last forever, I promise."

"I need the wind on my face. Please, isn't there some way you can let me sit outside, just for a few minutes."

Levi reached for her hand and took it between his.

"For you, I would sail to the ends of the earth, but Nathaniel would kill me if I took you out of this room."

Ginny pulled her hand from his and stormed to the trunk. She gathered the books in her arms and dumped them on the bed.

"Then I need more books to read."

He glanced at the pile and grinned, the humor dancing in his brown eyes. "You read all of them?"

"Twice." She folded her arms across her chest.

"Do you like science fiction?" he asked.

"I read *Frankenstein* and liked it. I'll read anything if you insist on keeping me in this room any longer."

Levi stood and collected the books in a neat stack.

"I'll see what I can find." He turned to go when she grabbed his sleeve.

"Where is Nathaniel?"

He looked perplexed for a moment. "Hasn't he returned?"

She shook her head. "Not since the night we left Alton."

A bark of laughter burst from Levi. He wagged his head as he caught his breath.

"I'll let him know you've inquired after him."

"Don't bother," she snapped, irritated for caring at all. "I hope he falls in the river and drowns."

"Careful what you wish for," he said before leaving the room.

Ginny groaned and stomped her feet. "Why do I even care about that man?"

Hours later, Ginny stirred to the sound of the lock turning and the door opening. She shifted beneath the blankets and peered through the darkness. Had she slept so long?

Thunk. The lid closed on the trunk. She turned toward it, rubbing the sleep from her eyes.

"Nathaniel?" she mumbled, trying to focus.

"I didn't mean to wake you. Go back to sleep." His voice echoed through the cabin, soothing and soft.

Ginny slipped from the bed and stood between him and the door. She placed her hand on the handle, blocking his escape.

"Virginia, what are you doing?" he asked.

She reached for him, her hand grasping the linen of his shirt. His sharp inhale made her look up. His features became clearer as her eyes accustomed to the darkness.

"Take me outside," she pleaded.

He sighed. "I can't do that."

"I'm begging you, please. I can't take being locked away in this room for one more day. I need to see the sky." She leaned against his chest. "I'll do anything. Anything."

He reached down and tipped her chin up. "You're still half asleep."

"I'm wide awake," she said with a frown.

Nathaniel put his hands on her arms and guided her back to bed.

"Go to sleep. I'll come speak to you in the morning."

"You won't. You haven't come to see me in days." She hesitated and spun around to face him. "Why? Am I that horrible that you can't stand to see my face?"

Nathaniel sighed again and reached for the lantern. Once he lit it, he turned to face her. The shirt he'd given her slid precariously off her shoulder. His gaze followed the line of buttons down to the hem of the shirt where it brushed against her bare legs.

"You're not wearing pants." He snatched the blanket off the bed and wrapped it around her.

"They itched and I couldn't sleep with them on."

His expression darkened, a stain of red climbing up his neck. "Virginia..."

"Yes, Nathaniel?" She blinked.

"Put some pants on," he said. "Now."

Without further instruction, he turned his back to her.

Ginny slipped into a pair of oversized trousers and fixed her shirt. After quickly braiding her loose hair over one shoulder, she tapped him on the back and sighed. "I've dressed."

Without turning around, Nathaniel opened the door to her room and glanced down the hallway. He snatched her wrist and dragged her toward a door at the far end of the hall. The sound of the paddlewheel grew louder with every step.

Excitement bubbled deep inside of Ginny.

When they reached the door, he opened it and peered outside. Her heart fluttered in her chest as he tugged on her hand and led her out onto the small platform beside the paddlewheel.

The sloshing and whirring of the wheel in the water blocked out the noise of the night around them. He led her to the port side of the ship and found a small alcove where they could stand and look out over the river without being spotted by anyone.

Her gaze focused on the shadows of the trees as they passed by. Virginia shivered as the cool air brushed against the bare skin of her neck. A pair of strong arms wrapped around her. The heat from his body sank into her. They stood for what seemed like hours. The sliver of moon peeked from behind clouds to cast minimal light on the river.

Virginia closed her eyes and leaned against him. His familiar scent mixed with the earthy river brought a comfort she hadn't felt since she'd last seen her family. A sob escaped her. The tears welled in her eyes, blurring the nighttime landscape.

His embrace tightened for the expanse of a breath and then he took her by the hand. Silently, he led her back inside to her cabin.

The sadness lingered even though the tears ceased. Ginny stared at Nathaniel, confused by the emotions churning in her heart. "Stay."

She gripped his hand tighter when he tried to let go.

Nathaniel pulled her into a gentle embrace. "I can't."

"I don't want to be alone. I...the..." She pursed her lips together, unable to say the word.

"Nightmares?" His voice held no judgment, only tenderness.

Ginny nodded.

He released her and crossed to the bed where the lantern hung. Once he blew out the flame, he climbed onto the bed, his back to the center.

"Lay, beneath the blankets."

Ginny quickly kicked off her shoes and scrambled onto the bed. She lay with her back to his. Although they didn't touch, she felt the heat from his body.

A few moments passed in silence. She wondered if he'd fallen asleep. The memory of being warm in his arms, the comfort and peace of being held, gave her confidence.

"Nathaniel?" she whispered.

"Yes."

"I'm cold."

He heaved a sigh. "Are you under the blankets?"

"Yes. I'm still cold. Can you warm me up?"

"You're testing my patience, Virginia."

"Please." She shivered in anticipation.

Nathaniel shifted his weight, and she heard the rustle of the blankets as he climbed beneath them. When his arm wrapped around her waist and he hauled her against him, Ginny could have cried out in relief. His warmth enveloped her a safe and warm cocoon. She felt his breath on her hair, the weight of his arm on her waist, his hand pressed against her stomach. Ginny wiggled against him in an attempt to get closer.

"Stop. Moving." He growled against her ear.

"I'm just getting comfortable."

"Every time you move, you make me uncomfortable," he snarled.

Virginia sighed and settled against him. Within moments, she felt the weight of worry fade away and smiled as she drifted off into the world of peaceful dreams.

Warmth surrounded him. Nathaniel snuggled closer to it. A wisp tickled his nose, and he twitched away. When he opened his eyes, he groaned.

Virginia lay tucked against him, her hair splayed on the pillow they shared. Her face inches from his. She looked so peaceful...her lips parted, her lashes lying delicately against her freckled cheek.

A grumbling snore came from her open mouth.

Nathaniel had to suppress the urge to laugh. He bit his lip and his tongue. *How could one graceless river rat have so much charm?* Without thinking, he reached up and pushed a curl away from her face.

She stirred, snuggling closer, licking her lips and sighing.

She's not yours. Nathaniel pulled his hand away.

Her eyes fluttered open, catching the stray rays of sunlight through the boarded window. When they focused on him, she sat up quickly taking the blanket with her.

"You're still here?"

With a sigh, Nathaniel got up. "Are you hungry?"

"I am." She dropped the blanket, revealing her rumpled shirt and a bare shoulder.

Damn. The innocence her expression held in sleep lingered still, even though she looked thoroughly debauched. Her curls mussed and hanging across her face, the flush of sleep along her cheek and down her neck. He wanted to push her down against that bed and make love to her.

Would her moans sound as sweet as her voice? He could make this little bird sing only for him. *Stop!* Nathaniel shook his head, chastising himself for thinking such things. His job was to protect her until he returned her to her family, not claim her.

Would that be so wrong? Nathaniel nodded to himself.

"Thank you." She blushed before climbing from the bed to fix her hair in the small mirror hanging on the wall.

"For what?" he asked, struggling to stop the unbidden desires raging in the back of his mind.

"Taking me outside, staying with me." She glanced at him in the mirror.

"I shall return in a few minutes." With a curt nod, he left her alone.

Once he'd slipped out into the hallway, he leaned his head against the door.

His body pulsed with awareness, with need, compulsions he recognized but often ignored. They were a day away from reaching Baton Rouge. He could control himself until they reached his home. Couldn't he?

"Good morning, Nathaniel."

Nathaniel straightened and turned to Levi who stood leaning against the wall, a smirk playing on his lips. "I pray you slept well last evening."

"I did."

"Did you keep her company through the night?" Levi grinned, his eyes sparkling with mischief.

"Where I sleep and whom I keep company are none of your concern, *Captain*," Nathaniel snapped.

Levi put his hands up. "I meant nothing by it. I'm just relieved to see the girl has finally received some of the attention she deserves."

"You've been spending time with her every day. Don't think that has escaped my notice."

"At least I've been visiting her...and feeding her." Levi stepped closer, his voice low. "You can't just lock her away and pretend she isn't there."

"I know full well she's there." Nathaniel growled.

"Why are you ignoring her then?"

Nathaniel raked his hand through his hair. "She's a distraction."

"You mean a temptation?"

He glared at his friend, setting his jaw and refusing to rise to the bait.

Levi grinned. "Don't pretend you haven't the faintest idea what I'm talking about. I've seen the way your expression changes when I mention her name."

"Do you want me to confess my attraction to her? Fine. I want her, but that's not the point. She's innocent and a woman like her has no place in my life."

"She's not Sarah."

"Damn it, Levi. I told you never to —"

"To mention her again...yeah, I know. But the truth is, that was eleven years ago. Let it go." Levi clapped his hand on his shoulder. "Virginia is different."

"I'm responsible for her. I can't betray that by taking advantage of her." Nathaniel paused.

Levi had been his friend since they'd met during the war. As an eighteen year old kid with no direction, they'd been fast friends, even though Levi hadn't been much older. He recognized the tone of Levi's voice as one borne of concern and friendship.

"I can't. Not when I'm positive I'm responsible for the chaos in her life." He shook his head. "That wouldn't be fair to her."

Levi nodded. "Just spend time with the girl. She needs a friend, someone to pass the time with. Don't push her away because you're unable to deal with your own shit."

The two of them walked down the hallway.

"Wait," Levi said as he ducked into his cabin. When he reemerged, he held a stack of books in his hands. "Give these to her." He dropped them in Nathaniel's arms.

"Are these new books? Did she read the other ones already?"

Levi laughed.

"Twice. She threw them at me and told me to get her more to read if she was to remain locked away." He arched his brow. "If you're wise, you'll sneak her out on the deck once in a while."

"I did." Nathaniel remembered the night before, how she leaned against him when they stood outside, letting the cool spring air and the moonlight soothe the restlessness.

"Really?" Levi asked, his eyes wide and mouth open in shock. "Perhaps I underestimated you." He picked up a plate of food and balanced it on top of the books. "Give her my breakfast as well."

With a parting nod, he left to return to his duties.

Nathaniel returned to the cabin where Virginia waited. Taking his time as to not drop the books or the food, he opened the door and stepped inside.

Virginia turned from the window where she was trying to peek through the cracks in the boards. "I just wanted to see where we were."

He set the plate of food on the bed and then laid the books next to it. "Somewhere on the Mississippi River, if I'm not mistaken."

"Ha ha." She mocked him. "Why do you have them boarded up?" she asked, peeking through one last time before walking away.

"Normally these rooms are used for cargo. I've debated putting bars on the windows, but the boards are easier to remove if I need to."

Nathaniel gestured to the plate.

Virginia's eyes widened and she smiled, revealing the joy he'd glimpsed before. "Thank you." She sat and devoured the contents of the plate.

"You were hungry." Nathaniel frowned. Perhaps he had been neglecting her in his vain attempt to put distance between them.

"Starving. But then again, my brothers always used to tease me that I could eat more than they could...combined." She lay back on the bed and sighed. "What I wouldn't give for a cup of coffee."

Nathaniel grinned at her simplistic desire. "I'll see what I can do."

She sat up quickly, her hair bouncing against her shoulders. "Really?"

He nodded, noting the glow in her cheeks and the delight

in her eyes. "I normally prefer tea, but I can ask Levi for some coffee if it will make your trip more pleasant."

Before he could blink, she threw herself off the bed and into his arms. He instinctively held her against him.

"I knew you weren't as bad as you claimed." She pulled away with a smirk.

"Don't test that theory, river rat." He straightened and tamped down the need clawing at his insides. "Levi has given you new books as well."

"Jules Verne!" Virginia read the titles and grinned like a child at Christmas. "Sherlock Holmes!" She plucked the volume from the pile and hugged it against her chest. "I will thank him later."

Nathaniel frowned and cleared his throat. "Is there anything else you require?"

Virginia flipped open the book and glanced over the open pages at him. "Anything?"

"Whatever you wish, I shall endeavor to provide it...within reason." He arched his brow in warning.

"A bath."

Nathaniel nearly choked. The image of her naked and up to her chin in a bathtub with bubbles nearly struck him dead. "A bath?"

"Yes, is that possible?" Virginia asked, hope glimmering in her eyes.

"Not until we reach Baton Rouge." He saw her hope disappear. "But once we dock, I shall take you somewhere you can bathe and find clothing more suitable."

She pulled at her shirt. "What's wrong with this?"

He forgot he hadn't told her of his plans. "Once we reach my home, I shall need to keep you close to protect you until we return to Alton."

"I can pretend to be one of your workers," she offered with a grin.

Nathaniel shook his head. "You look like a child as you are. I need you to be the woman beneath the tattered boy's clothes and ratty cap."

Virginia scowled. "They tried to make me into a lady at boarding school." She paused then spat, "I hated it. I hated the dresses, the powder, the shoes, the decorum, all of it. I'm not a lady."

"Perhaps you're not what society thinks a lady should be, but there is a woman beneath these clothes. I intend to bring her to light. With the right guidance, I think you'll discover a different side to yourself." Nathaniel smiled.

"You're just saying that to make me into something I'm not." She snapped the book closed.

"Virginia, will you at least give it a chance?" he pleaded. "For your own safety, I'm asking you to try this. As a woman, I can keep you by my side at all times, to protect you until I can take you home to your family."

"From who?" Virginia snapped. "And how do you even know if my family is still alive, if they're looking for me?" Her eyes filled with tears again.

"From everyone." *Including myself.* He sighed and ground his teeth together. "I've sent a man back to investigate what happened at your farm. I intend to have a report waiting for me once we reach Baton Rouge."

Her expression filled with hope once again as she turned her tearstained face up to meet his gaze. He saw the hesitation hidden there. "How can I trust what you say?"

He shrugged. "I can't offer you anything but my word. If you cooperate with me, I will do my best to ensure your family's safety and return you to them as quickly as possible." His heart twisted at the thought of her leaving him. He ignored it.

"I will try." She clutched the book tightly.

"That is all I ask." Nathaniel tipped his head. "I will leave you to your book."

Without wanting to prolong their argument, he left the room and made his way to the starboard bow.

As he looked out over the water, he took several deep

breaths to calm the riot raging in the pit of his gut. Since the war, Nathaniel wanted nothing more than to keep to himself, to build his fortune and push everyone else away. It was the main reason he'd left England. His family and childhood friends, none of them understood the driving force behind his need to be free of it all...to be free from the woman who'd ruined him. *Sarah.*

A vision of Sarah's golden curls, bright azure eyes, and insincere smile made his heart seize, but the image faded into a mess of auburn curls framing impossibly large green eyes and a smile full of innocence. *Virginia.* His heart lurched into a canter and gained speed with every stride.

Superstitious or not, Nathaniel couldn't deny the attraction or the powerful pull of her personality. So strong, and yet so delicate.

He hung his head. *What in the devil am I thinking?*

With strangled resolve, Nathaniel turned his face to the sky and caught sight of a hawk soaring overhead, solidifying his decision. *You cannot make a caged bird sing.*

CHAPTER FIVE

"Where is he?" Ginny grumbled as she paced the small cabin. Every so often she would pause and glance out the cracks in the boarded window. Night had fallen and the air had grown impossibly warm for late April, then she remembered...*Louisiana. I'm in Louisiana.*

A thrill of terror and excitement raced through her. This was supposed to be the last night of their journey. Levi had delivered her dinner and informed her they'd be docking just after dark.

Nathaniel had remained wary of the men working on the ship, striving to keep her presence hidden. But it seemed her pleas had effectively swayed him to allow her a bit more freedom.

That part bothered her. Why he'd held her that first night and yet he kept his distance since then? She felt a pang of longing, a need for that physical connection with him. Part of her wanted to ask him to join her, but the memory of the cold expression on his face made her pinch her lips together.

Ginny knew even voicing the words would sound inappropriate. *Nathaniel, sleep with me, hold me...kiss me.*

She shook her head. Where had that last part come from? She sighed, finished packing the last of his belongings into the trunk, and stacked the borrowed books on the nightstand by the bed. Her fingertips stroked the spine of *20,000 Leagues Under the Sea.*

A soft knock startled her. She turned to see the door swing open with Levi standing there, his hand resting on the knob.

"Are you coming?" he asked with a mischievous smile on his lips.

"Yes," Ginny replied quickly as she dashed from the room.

Levi followed her down the hall. He reached the door to the deck and opened it for her. "Go straight down the gangplank; a car will be waiting for you."

She turned and reached out to cup his bearded cheek. "Thank you, for everything."

His eyes sparkled in the dim lamplight.

"My pleasure, Virginia. If I can ever be of service, please let me know. If I'm not here, have my men send word to me. They'll know how to contact me."

"I will." She dropped her hand.

He smiled and glanced away. "Best you go now, before Nathaniel comes searching for us."

With a nod, Ginny slipped out the door and down the narrow walkway toward the car that waited. She sighed as her feet rested on the firm ground and glanced over her shoulder at the riverboat that had served as her home for the last week.

Levi waved from where he stood at the railing.

She returned the gesture and the mixture of fear and excitement swelled again, forming a mass of butterflies in her stomach.

"Shall we?"

Ginny spun to see Nathaniel waiting in the driver's seat of the car.

"Of course, anything to be off that blasted ship." She climbed into the passenger's seat and slammed the door.

He put the vehicle into drive and flicked on the headlights. They drove together in silence. The dirt road wove through a forest of large trees draped with moss hanging like Christmas tinsel. She admired the shadows it cast on the road. An eerie calm settled in the car. The open windows provided a lovely breeze that cooled her overheated skin.

"It's hot here, even at night." She turned toward Nathaniel.

"Welcome to the deep south, river rat." He chuckled, the sound refreshing and unexpected. "I should have warned you, but it wouldn't have done any good. One doesn't really know what to expect until one feels it for themselves."

She fanned herself. "I can't imagine how hot it gets in the summer."

"Sweltering," he replied. "But after a while, you get used to it."

"Are you?"

"Am I what?"

"Used to it?" Ginny watched him with unabashed curiosity.

"No. And I doubt I ever shall be."

"Does it get this hot in England?" Ginny asked before she could stop herself.

Nathaniel shook his head. "Never. For the first several years I lived in America, I wondered what kind of hell the southern states truly were to be so unrelenting in both temperature and humidity."

"Why didn't you stay in New York or one of the northern states?"

"The Mississippi River," he replied simply, as if it were the answer to all life's mysteries.

"I've lived on the river my entire life and I've never heard anyone say its name with such reverence and awe. Cursing it, yes, respecting it, yes, but revering it, no." Ginny crossed her arms and glanced out the window. Although she couldn't see the river anymore since they'd detoured away from it, she could still sense its presence. It pulsed through her. "But I can see why you'd love it. I know I do."

Nathaniel cleared his throat but didn't say anything.

"How long have you known Levi?" Ginny asked,

emboldened by his sudden honesty.

"Since the war. We were stationed together in France."

"The great war," Ginny murmured, her voice soft. "How old were you? What was it like?"

"Terrifying, gruesome, humbling, especially for an eighteen year-old who had more bravado than common sense." He focused his attention on the road, his grip tight on the wheel. "I begged my parents to let me enlist. They conceded, but within months of my assignment, the war ended. If it hadn't been for Levi, I'd have been another name on the memorial list."

"Are you both the same age?"

"No, Levi is older than me by three years. He'd already been wounded once by the time I'd met him. He was working in the war office for one of the generals at that point. When we met, he recruited me to work for him running correspondence between the commanders." Nathaniel paused for a moment. "Saved my life."

"How?" Ginny knew she was pushing his tolerance. Honestly, she didn't mean to pry, but this was the first moment since they'd met that he'd even offered the slightest information about himself. She craved more.

"The unit I'd been assigned to was slaughtered. Had I been with them, I would have too." He glanced at her.

"I'm sorry." Ginny looked out the front window and noticed the glow of a city before them. "You don't have to answer my questions."

"I want to." Nathaniel sped up as the dirt road ended and the blacktop began.

"Where are we going?" Ginny asked in an attempt to lighten the somber mood.

"To see a friend of mine."

"Who is he?"

"*Her* name is Pamela and she's a very dear friend of mine. I expect you to treat her with respect and give her your undivided attention." His voice grew stern.

"Why would you expect I do otherwise?" Ginny crossed her arms. "I'm not a wild animal."

"Your behavior upon our first meeting might suggest otherwise." He glanced at her.

"I can behave myself if I set my mind to it."

With a huff, she added, "If you want me to be nice to her, I will."

"And no rude comments. Keep your opinion to yourself, at least until I can speak to her first."

"Why are we going to see her again?"

"Because she can turn you into something resembling a lady."

Ginny harrumphed and turned away. "They tried to do so at the boarding school and failed miserably."

"So you said, but something must have stuck." He turned down a well-lit street.

Her attention was riveted to the buildings they passed. "I doubt it."

Nathaniel wove through the streets and came to a row of townhouses in a residential neighborhood. He parked the car in front of them and turned to Ginny. "I'm not asking you to become a socialite, but I need you to carry yourself as a fully grown, confident, self-aware woman of the world." His gaze slipped down to rake over her body then back to her face. "Can you at least attempt to fulfill that request for me?"

Ginny sighed. "I guess I can."

He opened the door, stepped around the car to open hers, and offered his hand. She slipped her hand in his and stepped from the cab.

"Thank you," she said as she released his hand.

"See, this isn't as difficult as you thought." He offered his arm. "Shall we?"

Feeling his solid arm linked in hers made her heart beat faster. She remembered the night he'd held her in his embrace until she'd fallen asleep. She longed for more.

Together, they ascended the staircase to the townhome's

large red door bearing the number eighty-six in bold gold plating. He knocked and Ginny cast a sidelong glance at him, admiring his smooth profile. *He shaved.*

Before she could comment, the door swung open. Ginny gasped when she saw the woman standing before them. Her dark eyes matched her Hispanic complexion. The light played off her hair, making it shimmer like the river at midnight on a moonless night. Her smile upon seeing Nathaniel softened her sharp features.

"Nathaniel, darling, this is a pleasant surprise." The woman opened her arms, and he embraced her, leaving Ginny feeling oddly bereft and a bit irritated.

"Pamela, you look like a goddess, as always."

"Flattery will get you everything, Nathaniel, it always has."

The tall, curvy woman wore a red corseted silk evening gown with gold and black embroidery. Her breasts were neatly displayed in a heart shaped neckline with delicate straps draping across her shoulders. A fine black lace shawl lay over them. She stepped aside and gestured with her well-manicured hand.

"Come in, won't you?"

Ginny flinched when she stepped into the parlor. The scent of perfume overwhelmed her. Her gaze flickered to Pamela and then her surroundings. Ornate, rich décor in vibrant colors. Dark woods and plush fabrics. She should have known the moment she smelled the sickeningly sweet scent that this was a den of sin.

She'd read about them and heard the stories from her brothers, but never had she dreamed she'd be standing in the parlor of a brothel. Her family would kill her if they ever found out. Ginny glanced up at Nathaniel who stood beside her, his attention on Pamela, but she felt the solid weight of his hand against the base of her spine.

"Nathaniel, it's been months since you've last graced us with your presence." Pamela motioned for them to follow her into the parlor. "Come have a drink."

The parlor boasted extravagant décor to match the entryway. Ginny nearly gagged at the opulence. The country suffered the ravages of a depression and yet this kind of extravagance had found a way to exist. She nearly scowled at the woman.

"Who is this young man?" Pamela asked, handing Nathaniel a crystal glass with clear liquid in it.

Nathaniel removed Ginny's cap with his free hand and her hair spilled out over her shoulders. Ginny leveled a glare at him.

Pamela shrieked.

"Oh sweet merciful heavens, what in the devil have you done?" Pamela's expression went ashen as her gaze flickered between Nathaniel and Ginny.

"I shall explain in a moment, but I will admit to there being an ulterior motive for me coming to you tonight." He reached for her hand and clasped it between his. "I need a favor."

The color returned to Pamela's cheeks, although her red lips were parted in shock.

"It takes a lot to unman me like this, Nathaniel." She straightened and took a deep breath. "I already have my hands full trying to keep the cops from raiding my establishment. I'm not willing to put my girls in danger any more than I have to."

"I'm not asking you to put yourself or your girls in danger." Nathaniel released her hand to rest his hands on Ginny's shoulders. "I need you to turn her into a lady."

When Pamela burst into laughter, Ginny wanted to deck her. Nathaniel's grip tightened on her shoulders, as though he could sense her intention. She glanced up at him. His mismatched eyes glinted with warning and he shook his head. Ginny crossed her arms and stared at the madam.

"You want me to turn this bedraggled tomboy into a lady?" Pamela stopped laughing long enough to peer at

Ginny carefully. "Do you think I'm a miracle worker? I'm good, Nathaniel, but this would take an act of God, or Congress."

Ginny pinched her lips together lest she open her mouth and let the woman before her have both barrels of her good opinion. But she had promised Nathaniel she would attempt to show some decorum, so she bit her tongue.

"Can you do this or not?" he asked, a slight irritation in his tone.

"What's in it for me?" Pamela purred, licking her lower lip as she met his gaze.

Ginny nearly vomited.

"I will compensate you handsomely for your time and any expenses that should arise from her tutelage." He straightened and glanced at Ginny, offering a smile.

Pamela tapped a glossy fingernail against her cheek as if pondering the situation. The wheels were churning in her head, Ginny could see it, but she would take his offer. Women like her were nothing if not predictable. Ginny rolled her eyes.

"Pamela, will you do this for me?" Nathaniel asked with growing impatience.

With a heavy sigh, Pamela relented. "I'll do it. But you owe me, Nathaniel Blackthorne."

He grinned and released Ginny to shake Pamela's hand. "How long do you need?"

"A week."

"You have three days." Nathaniel released her hand when Pamela nodded. A look of relief on his face, he glanced down at Ginny. "I shall return, until then you'll stay here with Pamela. Do not leave this house, do you understand? Better yet, keep to your room."

"Can't I come with you?" Ginny asked.

"You're in good hands here. I promise." He put his hat on and walked toward the door. "Pamela, if any harm comes to her, I will take it out of your hide."

The glorious madam arched her brow and waved as he

walked out the door. Then she turned to Ginny with a sigh. "The things I do for that man. Well, c'mon, sugar, let's burn those rags and see what I have to work with." She snatched Ginny by the wrist and dragged her up the stairs.

Ginny went willingly, amazed the woman could walk in the shoes she wore. As they reached the top of the stairs, several doors opened revealing women of varying sizes and ethnicities. They watched with curious eyes as Pamela led her down the hall and up a second flight of stairs.

When they reached the landing, Pamela flicked on a light revealing a lavish bedroom with jewel toned silks and velvets. The grand wrought iron bed in the corner matched the makeup vanity and end tables.

"Don't just stand there with your mouth hanging open." She turned to enter a small room tucked off to the left. "Come in and close the door behind you."

Ginny did as she was asked. She stood in the center of the room, feeling as though she'd somehow stepped into another century. Even the rooms at the boarding school and her aunt's home, had not seemed so extravagant or elegant.

The sound of water running snapped Ginny from her awe. Pamela stepped back into the room.

"I'll let you have my room for the few days you're here." She waved her hand. "The toilet is in here. I've taken the liberty of drawing a bath for you."

"I've been dying for one." Ginny could have sighed in relief. She'd washed herself with a rag for the last two weeks. Sinking into a tub of hot water sounded divine.

Pamela stepped forward and toyed with the wild curls hanging over Ginny's shoulders. "We'll have to see what we can do about your hair. Have you any aversion to cutting it?"

Ginny shook her head. "Hair grows back, and to be honest, I've wanted to cut it for ages. The ladies at the boarding school told me it would make me more wanton to give into the current styles."

"Stuff and nonsense." Pamela snorted in disapproval as

she stepped up to a closet and removed a few articles of clothing as well as a lovely cream-colored gown. "Take a bath. I shall lay out some clothes for you to wear as well as a nightgown. Tomorrow, we can discuss your schooling and how I can help you further blossom."

"Thank you." The disgust Ginny had first felt upon arrival disappeared.

"I'm not sure what Nathaniel has planned, sugar. But I've never had him request a favor quite like this from me before." She arched her brow. "He must see something in you, which frankly shocks me considering his history with Sarah."

Ginny stood there, unsure what to say in response and a bit confused. *Who the hell is Sarah?* She nodded and offered a small smile instead of voicing her curiosity.

"Stay in this room. I shall return to bring you breakfast in the morning." Pamela pushed her toward the sound of running water. "Use the lemon verbena, it'll make your hair shine." With that, she closed the door of the small bath room.

The sight of the water with the steam curling up made her sigh. Ginny stripped quickly and stepped into the scalding water. As she sank down, her body screamed in delight.

While she lounged in the water, her mind wandered to Nathaniel and Pamela's comment. *He must see something in you.* Surely Pamela was mistaken. As much as Ginny longed for Nathaniel's attentions, he played the perfect gentleman, seeing to her needs, protecting her with the promise to return her to her family. She sighed.

"If only I knew I had a family to return to..." she mumbled before shaking her head. "I will not dwell on the possibilities, not until I know for certain." After snatching the soap, she began to scrub herself clean and then dipped beneath the water in order to wash her hair.

Sufficiently cleaned and refreshed, Ginny stepped from the bath and wrapped a plush towel around her body. She padded into the bedroom after peeking inside and finding it vacant.

A lovely silk nightgown lay on the bed along with a matching robe. Ginny let her fingers glide over the material. Soft and decadent. She removed the towel and slipped the garment on, savoring the slide of the fabric against her bare skin. A moan escaped her.

"A girl could get used to this," she murmured, grabbing the towel and drying her hair before it could dampen the material further.

She sat at the vanity and brushed her hair, carefully untangling and then braiding the mass. The multicolored strands glittered. Pamela had been right; the lemon made it shine.

"But can she do the same with me?"

Nathaniel stepped into his club with a nod to the tall, broad-shouldered man standing by the door. "Evening, Carl."

"Good evening, Mr. Blackthorne. It's good to see you've returned." He offered a wide smile.

"Feels good to be back. Any problems while I was gone?" he asked, letting his gaze skim over the patrons.

"Only one, sir." Carl nodded to the bartender. "Thomas and I have tried to be vigilant. Might want to ask him about the details though, sir."

"I shall. Thank you, Carl." Nathaniel clapped his hand on his friend's shoulder and crossed the room to where his office door blended into the décor almost seamlessly.

The music drifting from the stage soothed as well as entertained. His gaze lingered on the band playing an upbeat melody with an undercurrent of soul. Jazz had exploded in popularity, and Nathaniel had the nagging intuition to capitalize on the craze. It had served him well. The problem had become finding performers who were both trustworthy and talented. Since the start of the depression, he'd found more who were willing to break the law, if only to feed their families.

Nathaniel's clientele often extended into the wealthy and privileged. He capitalized on their selective and often expensive tastes. The Casa de Luna served as not only a lucrative business for him, but a bottomless pit of invaluable resources. The cream of Baton Rouge spent their time drinking at his establishment. Lucrative indeed.

The bartender, Thomas, approached him. "Sir, if I might have a word?"

"Yes, Thomas, what is it?"

"They've been asking for Dixie."

"Well, put her on stage next." Nathaniel glanced up, his brow furrowed at the mention of their most popular singer.

"That's the problem, sir. See, she disappeared while you were gone."

"She what?" Nathaniel's grip tightened on the door handle.

"About a week ago, she disappeared. Never showed up for her curtain call. I sent Carl to check on her, but the house was empty." Thomas shrugged. "We've been relying on the band since then and I think the patrons are quickly losing interest, sir. They want something fresh."

Nathaniel nodded. "I understand. Thank you for telling me, Thomas. I shall see what I can arrange."

Thomas returned to his duties leaving Nathaniel to ponder this latest conundrum. He pushed open the door to his office and closed it behind him as he flicked on the light. The warmth of familiarity calmed him.

He sat in the oversized chair behind the oak desk where a stack of papers and days of correspondence lay. Tapping his fingers against his thigh, he sighed. Normally he would have dived headfirst into work, but the news about Dixie had thrown his mind into disarray. Well, he was already distracted with thoughts of Virginia.

Had it been wise to leave her with Pamela? If he'd have brought her here, she'd have stood out like a manure pile in Buckingham Palace. He shook his head. Of course he'd done the right thing. Pamela wouldn't dare cross him, not with their history. She was as loyal to him as Levi.

Nathaniel groaned and opened the bottom drawer of his desk. He withdrew a small decanter as well as a single glass. Amber liquid swirled in the crystal and his mouth watered. He poured a finger's worth of liquid into the glass and then replaced the decanter before closing the drawer. Nathaniel brought the glass to his nose and inhaled, savoring the rich, familiar scent.

When the liquid touched his lips and slid across his tongue, he groaned. Nothing, not even the finest moonshine or the smoothest rum, could compete with the delightful aromatic ecstasy of whisky... Not hooch, not brown, but authentic Scottish whisky. His eyes closed as the alcohol slid down his throat, warming him from the inside. He leaned back in his chair, the glass cradled in his hand.

He sighed and glanced at the liquor.

"I suppose I'll have to make the journey then, if only to have you close by." He chuckled. "I must be losing it if I'm talking to the whisky that way." He set the glass down. The amount in the decanter was all that remained of the case he'd shipped with him eleven years ago.

A soft knock brought a welcome reprieve.

"Enter," he said, not bothering to hide the glass or the liquor contained therein.

The door opened and Nathaniel stood when he saw Levi standing there. "Has something happened?"

Levi closed the door behind him and took off his cap. "No, but I wanted to deliver this in person." He held out a letter.

Nathaniel took it and tore the envelope open. He glanced through the contents, his fears confirmed with every line. He noted the signature of his lawyer, C.R. Evans, at the bottom with a request for further instructions. With a sigh, he folded the letter and tucked it into his pocket.

"Was that the report from the man I sent back to Alton?" Levi asked, stepping closer and leaning his hands on the desk.

"Yes, he did well by relaying his report through Evans." Nathaniel nodded, his thoughts lost on what to do next.

"Nathaniel, talk to me. What the hell is going on?"

"Her oldest brother escaped with the three youngest. The other two have disappeared."

"Heaven have mercy," Levi whispered. "What of her father?"

Nathaniel shook his head and collapsed in the chair. "Shot." He pointed to his head.

"Son of a bitch." Levi raked his hand across his beard. "What are you going to tell her?"

"I think she deserves the truth, even though it will crush her. She deserves to know."

Levi nodded. "What do you need me to do?"

A hundred thoughts flooded Nathaniel at once. He picked up the whisky and drained the glass.

"Finish the job I gave you. The run to New Orleans, I need that shipment." He paused for a moment. "I'll have Evans find a place for the four siblings and hire a detective to find the missing ones."

"Why are you doing this? It's not like this was your fault."

Nathaniel glanced up at Levi, a pit of regret in his stomach. "Yes, it is."

"I'll be back in a few days," Levi snapped. He pulled his cap on and left Nathaniel without another word.

"How the hell am I going to tell her?" He pulled the decanter from the drawer and poured another glass. "I'm going to break her heart."

CHAPTER SIX

Ginny tugged at the shimmering fabric. It was too tight. She wasn't used to constricting clothes and missed the comforting embrace of her trousers.

Pamela had given her an entire wardrobe of lovely, feminine dresses, including a trousseau of undergarments and shoes to match each one. Ginny had never felt so uncomfortable in her life, not even when she'd been at the boarding school. These clothes went beyond lady and into decadent. Pamela had taken Nathaniel at his word when he'd given her carte blanche.

They'd spent the last three days addressing and refreshing rules of etiquette and decorum. Which seemed laughable considering they were being taught by a high class madam.

She looked in the mirror and spun around, mesmerized by the twirl of the skirt. The deep indigo satin hugged every curve. Curves she hadn't realized she'd had. The glitter of the fabric under the dim lights made it look like starlight shimmering beneath the dark purple hues. The neckline dipped into a vee, stopping just above her breasts. It showed her cleavage. Cleavage she'd been wise to hide for all those years beneath boy's clothes. Had her brothers...her father...ever seen how feminine she truly was, they'd have locked her in the attic and never let her out for fear of someone stealing her away.

The makeup smoothed her complexion, highlighting her high cheekbones accented by a hint of rouge. The dark liner brought emphasis to her green eyes. She pouted, unsure of the red lipstick. It was truly her hair, or lack thereof, that made the most pronounced statement. Pamela had cut it short in a tapered bob that lay just below her bare shoulders, smoothed with crème to tame the curls and shape it into a fashionable updo.

Her reflection revealed another person altogether. Ginny looked like a woman, a bona fide, hot-blooded woman.

Ginny frowned. What if Nathaniel didn't like it? She hoped he appreciated her effort. A small piece of her wanted to make him happy, in an effort to show him some kind of gratitude for all the trouble she'd put him through. Ginny bit her lip, nervous she would disappoint him...and herself.

Pamela reappeared in the doorway, pausing just inside the door with a Cheshire smile on her lips. Ginny hesitated for a moment, unsure if her expression was good or not.

"Sugar, you look like a dream," Pamela said, slipping up beside her. "Nathaniel is going to love all my hard work."

Ginny shot her a look, complete with arched brow. The woman really did have no shame, but she couldn't really argue with the madam's innate sense of style. Ginny shook her head.

"Now don't do that." She smoothed a stray curl behind Ginny's ear. "I worked extra hard to get that wild hair of yours to curl just right. Wouldn't want to mess it up before the big reveal, would we? He's downstairs waiting for you."

A flurry of nervous energy balled in the pit of her stomach. "He's here?"

"Yes." Pamela took her by the arm. "Come, let's not keep your patron waiting."

Together they descended the stairs. Ginny took her time, both to avoid the inevitable and to keep from falling flat on her face. She hated heeled shoes. When they reached the main landing, she glanced up to see Nathaniel standing at the bottom of the stairs, his back to them.

"Nathaniel," Pamela called out in a singsong voice.

He turned around and his eyes widened when they rested on Ginny. Heat rose along her neck and into her cheeks. Embarrassed, she turned her gaze to the steps until she reached the ground floor.

"Doesn't she look lovely?" Pamela asked with a hint of pride in her voice.

When she raised her eyes, Nathaniel's expression startled her. His lips were pressed tightly together, his eyes dark and unreadable.

"You're not leaving this house dressed like that." His words were clipped, tight, as though attempting to harness something deeper and darker than could be voiced aloud.

Ginny tipped up her chin. "I thought you wanted me to be a lady."

"A lady, yes," he said in a low voice, "not a goddamned temptress." He snatched a flimsy lace shawl from Pamela's outstretched hand and wrapped it around her shoulders. "I'd rather you change, but we need to leave. I'm already late."

He took her by the arm and pulled her from the house, leaving a slack-jawed Pamela staring after them.

When they stepped out into the evening air, Ginny turned her face up to the sky. The breeze whispered across her skin and she sighed.

Nathaniel led her down the stairs and opened the car door. She climbed in, wincing when he slammed it shut.

"What in the devil..." she murmured as he rounded the car and climbed into the driver's seat.

He refused to look at her as he threw the car into gear and sped off. Ginny gripped the door and the seat. They drove in silence for a few moments before she lost all patience with him.

"Nathaniel, slow down!"

He didn't respond, but the car's speed declined to a reasonable pace.

"Is something wrong?" she asked, searching his profile.

"Nothing is amiss, if that's what you're asking." He

glanced at her then back to the road. "But you...that...is all kinds of wrong."

Ginny glanced down at herself. "What?"

A sharp turn took them down a dirt road. When he didn't respond, Ginny focused her attention to the dark scenery as it passed by. She caught a glimpse of the moonlight as it flashed between the trees. Concentrating on something concrete, something real, helped her cope with the nagging in the back of her mind. *Does he not like how I look now? Why should I even care? Pamela only dressed me like this because he requested it.* Ginny crossed her arms and ignored him.

When the river came into view, Ginny stared at it with longing, suddenly overwhelmed by homesickness. She missed her family. Fanning her eyes, she willed herself not to cry, lest it smear her makeup. Pamela had warned her about tears being the worst enemy of a glamorous woman.

They drove along until Nathaniel pulled up to a small dock by the river. Before he could turn off the ignition, Ginny threw open the door and escaped the car's confines. She righted herself and carefully made her way to the dock.

The moon shone brightly overhead, nearly full. Her heels clicking on the wood and the sound of nighttime creatures the only indication of life. She stood on the end of the dock, her face turned up to the moon, admiring the bright glow and the twinkle of the stars surrounding it.

Nathaniel's steps echoed behind her, but she refused to turn to face him. The last three days...no, the last week and a half she'd done whatever he'd requested, and for what? To feel the sting of rejection as he criticized her effort. She pulled the shawl tighter.

"Virginia."

His voice melted into her, but she remained steadfast, keeping her back to him.

"Penny for your thoughts."

"Just admiring the river," she lied. "It looks like blue ink."

He chuckled. "I wondered that before, but not about this river. The Thames. When I was a child, I remember asking my mother if it would cling to you like ink, staining your skin if you went in the water after dark."

"I miss doing that."

"Doing what?" he asked.

"Swimming by moonlight." She sighed.

Nathaniel didn't respond, just stood behind her, a presence of both comfort and confusion.

"Back home we have a small pond behind the house. It's fed by a spring." She paused. "I used to sneak out of the house on hot, clear summer nights, when the moon is full and high. I would slip out of my clothes and jump right in. Didn't test the water first, I just jumped." Her eyes drifted closed at the memory.

He took a deep breath beside her, but said nothing.

"It was like diving into a cooling bath. The water so dark it looked like a bottomless void." Her heart beat faster as she confessed to him. Why was she telling him this anyway? "I never got caught, although Michael found me sneaking home one night." She chuckled.

"You swam naked by moonlight?" Nathaniel asked, his voice low.

Ginny turned to look at him, his expression shadowed by the darkness and a hunger that surprised her. "Yes, especially when it got hot and sticky during the summer."

His eyes darkened, if that were possible. She cocked her head and studied him.

"Virginia." He took her by the shoulders, the heat of his hands seeping through the flimsy lace and burning her skin.

She missed his touch, the sound of his voice, his scent, the way she fit in his embrace.

"I did what you asked me," she said. "I tried to listen and learn and I tried damn hard to be a lady." Ginny wanted to stomp her feet and poke her finger in his chest, but she stood still, her breaths coming in pants as he scowled at her. "I tried.

It's not my fault you don't like what you see. Blame Pamela, blame yourself, but stop treating me like I did something wrong."

Nathaniel laughed and shook his head. "I do blame myself, more than you know."

"Then why..."

"I'm a fool. A ridiculous, blind fool." He raked his hand through his hair and stepped away. His tongue wet his lips as he stared out over the water. "We should go. We were supposed to be at the club an hour ago."

Ginny blinked, a sudden wave of regret and disappointment surging through her. *What is he talking about? And why is my heart racing?* When she saw him lick his lips, her body flared to life. She wanted to kiss him. But the moment had passed. Regret settled like a stone in her gut.

He took her arm and led her back to the car. They drove a short distance to a small building just inside the city. It looked like Pamela's townhome, but the façade boasted more masculine accents and a darker paint. He parked the car in the back alley.

The two of them approached the back door. Nathaniel knocked twice. An older woman answered.

"Hello, Nana." He took off his hat and greeted the woman.

"Go ahead, Nathaniel." She gestured with her arm, her gaze brushing over Ginny as she passed.

"Where are we going?" Ginny asked as Nathaniel opened a door leading down a set of dark basement stairs.

"You'll see."

When they reached the bottom, he knocked on the door three times. It opened to reveal the largest black man Ginny had ever seen.

"Mr. Blackthorne, welcome." He opened the door wider and gestured in invitation.

"This is Virginia," Nathaniel said as they stepped inside.

The man guarding the door smiled at her. "Lovely to

meet you, miss. I'm Carl."

"Hello, Carl." She nodded, immediately at ease from his warm greeting.

"Enjoy your evening," he said as he resumed his post.

"Thank you," she replied over her shoulder as Nathaniel led her into the room. When she turned around, she gasped in surprise.

The basement had been transformed into another world. A large stage sat at the center where a band played a slow jazz tune. Hardwood tables with chairs dotted the floor surrounding an open space in the center of the room. Every table seated to full capacity, the patrons sipping drinks from glittering crystal glass. To her right stood a rich mahogany bar with a shining mirror glinting behind it manned by a dark haired bartender with a curved mustache. He nodded when she spied him.

"Nathaniel, where are we?" she whispered.

"My club, Casa de Luna." His hand closed over hers where it rested on his arm. "What do you think?"

Ginny took in the opulence and blinked as some of the patrons turned to look at them. "I think you're the one keeping secrets, Nathaniel," she whispered.

He led her to a door next to the bar. When he opened the door, she entered the room first. The scent of tobacco and leather with a hint of citrus welcomed her. Then she noticed the masculine furniture and a stack of papers on the large oak desk.

"Is this your office?" she asked.

"It is." He closed the door behind him.

"Why did you bring me here?"

"I need to keep you close. Pamela said you were going stir crazy locked in her room. So I decided to bring you here while I worked." He leaned against the desk.

"Really?" Ginny could hear the soft strains of the music through the wall. "What do you want me to do then while you work? I can't just sit here and stare at you."

Nathaniel straightened. "No, I do have something you can do for me."

"Yes?" She crossed her arms under her breasts.

He frowned as his gaze lingered on her chest. She immediately dropped her arms to her sides.

"I'm not used to these clothes." She brushed the skirt with her gloved hand.

"They look lovely on you." He cleared his throat. "How do you feel about performing?"

Ginny's gaze snapped up. "Like acting?" Fear settled in her stomach.

"Like singing." Nathaniel shifted his weight. "Our headliner left us without a replacement. They're desperate for some new entertainment."

"You want me to go on stage and sing? Here? Now?" Panic swelled deep inside of her.

"Yes. I've heard you sing. They'll love you."

Ginny toyed with the hem of her shawl. "I don't know. I've never sung in front of anyone except for my family before." She waved her hand. "I mean I tried to once at boarding school. I ended up heaving all over the stage. It wasn't pretty."

Nathaniel came up to her and rested his hands on her arms. "Look at me."

She met his gaze. "I'm not..."

"You're perfect," he whispered before leaning down to press a kiss to her forehead. "I wouldn't ask you to do it if I didn't have faith in you."

Ginny nodded while her heart sang at his praise and the simple kiss. She shook her head free of the childish reaction and put a finger up between them. "One song. That's it. And only tonight."

Nathaniel's grin made her heart pound.

Simple girl, letting him affect you so with merely a smile. Ginny stepped away from him.

"Come on, let's get this over and done."

Nathaniel took her to the door leading back stage. What had possessed him to ask her to sing? When he'd seen her descend the stairs at Pamela's, he thought his heart had stopped. She looked elegant and regal, almost angelic. His body reacted to her before he could register the reality that the woman coming toward him was the same girl who'd stowed away in his trunk.

He'd wanted to hide her away from the world even more. The gown revealed just enough skin to entice, and the makeup enhanced her natural beauty, making her look older and more seductive. It had taken all of his effort to not wrap his arms around her and kiss those luscious lips. He'd wanted her before, but he'd been able to control himself. Seeing her transformed into a sensual woman only added gasoline to the fires raging inside of him.

She stopped beside him off to the side of the stage behind the large velvet curtains. Her hands twisted in her skirts and she chewed on her lower lip as she gazed out over the crowd from the shadows.

"I don't know if I can do this, Nathaniel. What if I get sick? What if they hate me?" she whispered, pressing her hand to her throat.

He took her hand in his. "They'll love you." Her hand trembled in his, so he held it tighter. "You'll be magnificent."

"What should I sing? I don't know anything new and fashionable." She turned her wide eyes to him in panic.

"Sing whatever is in your heart; the band will pick it up once you begin." He gathered her in his arms. "Pretend I'm the only person in the audience, Virginia. Sing for me...only me."

She pulled away to glance up at him. "Sing for you?"

"I'll be sitting at the bar in the back, watching you. Just know I'm there and you'll be fine."

He released her, unable to contain his body's reaction to her proximity. Her sweet scent teased his nose, toying with his mind. The soft press of her curves against him drove him mad with longing. He had to put distance between them, for her sake.

Ginny took a deep breath and exhaled. She repeated this several times until the soft strains of the current song ended.

"I'll introduce you."

"All right," she whispered.

Nathaniel stepped past her onto the stage.

"Good evening, ladies and gentlemen. Unfortunately, our lovely singer, Dixie, has moved on to bigger and brighter adventures. But, don't count your misfortunes too quickly, for on my journeys I have discovered a lovely songbird and brought her here just for your listening enjoyment. May I introduce the Nightingale of New Orleans."

The room filled with applause and murmurs as Virginia tiptoed onto the stage. Nathaniel took her hand and kissed the backs of her fingers, meeting her gaze. He smiled in an effort to soothe her nerves. She returned his smile and he saw the tension in her expression fade. When he released her hand, she stepped forward and wrapped her hand around the microphone stand.

"Good evening." Virginia's voice echoed through the room.

Nathaniel disappeared backstage, stopping just behind the curtain before turning to watch her.

The stage lights caught the fine silver threads of her gown, making the indigo shine and sparkle. Her expression softened as she closed her eyes. Then she opened her mouth, and the whole world went silent.

A soft melody, enchanting and beautiful, flowed from her lips. An old song, but one with heart and depth of soul. The band picked up within a few bars, filling in the instrumental to compliment her vocals. She put her heart into it, almost as if every ounce of her being came out in that song.

Nathaniel stood there, enraptured by the power of her voice. He'd overheard her singing on the ship, but he'd never imagined the immensity of it until that very moment. Shaking his head, he turned from the stage and smoothed his hand over his hair. He slipped out the door and made his way to the bar.

The sweet allure of her voice followed him as he approached Thomas, who was leaning on the bar, his jaw hanging open. When he saw Nathaniel, Thomas straightened and grabbed a rag to wipe the polished mahogany counter.

With a half-hearted glance over his shoulder, Nathaniel caught sight of the woman who had completely consumed him. He had tried to push thoughts of her away, tried to resume his daily routine, but he found himself distracted constantly. Hearing her sing on his stage only solidified it. He had to find somewhere else for her to stay until he found a way to reunite her family.

He combed his hand through his hair again. Nathaniel couldn't even bring himself to tell her what had happened that day. She would break in two if she knew her father was dead. He would tell her, but not until the time was right, once he had news of her brothers and confirmation of their safety.

"Can I get you something, Nathaniel?" Thomas asked. "You look distracted."

"Yeah. Give me a rum." Nathaniel leaned on the bar watching Virginia in the mirror behind it.

"Where did you find her?" Thomas set the glass on the bar in front of him.

"On the river," he replied as he lifted the rum to his lips. The sweet, smooth burn of the liquor took the edge off, but he knew even a whole bottle wouldn't wash away the need simmering in the pit of his gut.

"It's like listening to an angel." Thomas leaned closer. "She's entranced them. Look."

Nathaniel reluctantly turned around again. Sure enough, the entire audience seemed frozen in time, barely breathing, watching Virginia. He knew she would be a sensation. With a nod, he spun around to face Thomas again.

"I'm not surprised." He tapped the glass again, and Thomas filled it. "She has that effect on people."

"You'd best keep a close eye on her. She'll attract quite a bit of attention now."

"I had no intention of letting her wander." Nathaniel downed the liquid in one shot. The alcohol cleared his head, but his heart grew heavy with the knowledge that in a few weeks she would be gone.

The song came to an end and applause erupted. Everyone rose to their feet, catcalls and cheers raised as Virginia bowed to them and stepped backstage.

The band struck up another song and the applause gave way to murmured conversation. While some of the customers resumed their seats, some decided to dance. It seemed the spell Virginia had cast slowly disintegrated.

He saw her step from the stage door and walk toward him. Her eyes glowed with pride and determination. Several of his guests stepped into her path, effectively stopping her. Their animated gestures and her laughter assured him of an innocent conversation. She looked up for a moment, catching his gaze and smiling.

He nodded in response and turned to Thomas. "Keep an eye on her. Serve her only water, that's an order." Nathaniel sighed as more people surrounded her. "I'll be in my office."

"Yes, sir."

"Tell Carl to keep a sharp eye as well."

Thomas nodded.

Nathaniel slipped into his office without a final look at Virginia. His heart swelled at the thought of her brimming with joy, but he couldn't bear to see her among the crowd, talking with other men. If he remained to watch her himself, he'd cause a scene. And that would most definitely not be good for business.

He shut the door and crossed to his desk, reaching for the

decanter. After pouring the remaining liquid into his glass, he collapsed on the chaise lounge and propped his feet up.

"She's not yours. You don't need her. She'll only bring you heartache," he murmured to himself. "Remember what Sarah did? She made you feel the same way...like you couldn't live without her."

The swirling liquid called to him. He took a sip, trying to drown the memory of the woman who'd broken his heart. Another followed in an attempt to bury the need for Virginia.

All he had to do was wait. Wait for Evans to find her brothers. Then he would set them up on a nice little farm and leave them in peace. It was the least he could do, considering what his presence in their life had cost them.

The evidence hadn't been clear in Evan's letter, but there was no doubt in his mind that the Garrett brothers were behind the attack on her family. They must have followed him when he went to talk to Mr. Chapman. He took another drink and leaned his head back against the chaise.

Virginia had to have seen something that day. He knew he had to ask her again, to know for sure who had done this. But if he asked her, it would lead to the inevitable truth about her father.

He took another drink, nearly choking when there was a knock at the door. Nathaniel coughed and sat up. "Come in," he gasped, still trying to clear his throat.

The door opened and Virginia stepped into his sanctuary. "Sorry to disturb you," she said as she closed the door behind her and leaned against it.

He had to give Pamela credit. The shade of the gown perfectly highlighted Virginia's features, accenting her curves and casting a near regal bearing on her. She stole his breath away, just as she had earlier when he'd seen her at Pamela's home.

"Do you need something, Virginia?" He stood and set his empty glass on the desk.

His gaze roamed over her. She walked like a lady, talked

like a lady, but her eyes still held that fire he knew simmered just below the surface. Yes, Pamela was most certainly a miracle worker. No one would recognize her as the mousey little river rat from Alton, Illinois.

"I just wanted to know what you thought of my song," she said, a blush staining her cheeks.

A pang of desire struck him in the chest at her innocent statement. He had to turn away, lest his state of arousal be completely obvious to her. He leaned against the desk and counted to ten in his mind.

"Did I make a mess of it?" she asked.

When he turned around, she stood there with her hip thrust out and her hand resting on top of it, her gaze narrowed. His little river rat shone through the trappings and the contrast made him smile.

He fixed a stack of papers before turning back to her. "You did fantastic, kid, just like I said you would. Did you enjoy being on stage?"

She shifted her weight again, dropping her hands to her sides. "Yes...and no." Virginia toyed with the hem of the shawl. "Singing in front of everyone like that, hearing their applause, it made my heart soar. Even hearing the compliments from people when I left the stage...it felt good to know I could offer something people would enjoy."

"But?" he pressed, recognizing the conflicting emotions in her actions.

"I'm not used to that kind of attention." She met his gaze. "I mean they were polite. The ladies complimented my voice, and the men fawned over me, offering to buy me drinks and join them for dances." Virginia shrugged.

"Did they hurt you?" He reached out and tipped up her chin so he could gauge her expression accurately. Her skin slid soft against his fingertips. Her green eyes rimmed with black liner were shadowed by the lighting.

"No, no one hurt me." She studied his face. "I just...I'm not used to being in that position."

"Do you not care for their attention?" he asked.

"Theirs?" She paused stepping closer. "No."

"I promise, you don't have to sing again if it makes you that uncomfortable."

"I only sang because you asked me to." She rested her palm against his chest, and Nathaniel froze, his body heating beneath her touch. "You asked me to sing for you."

"I would never force you to do anything, Virginia. You know this."

Her heeled shoes gave her some height, but she still had to tilt her head back to look up at him. She slid her hand up to encircle his neck.

Nathaniel swallowed hard, holding his breath. Her fingertips toyed with the hair lying against his collar.

"Virginia," he whispered as she leaned closer.

Her gentle hand pulled his head down. He thought about fighting it, but her scent wrapped around him like a snare, pulling him toward his fate. Her breath brushed across his lips. He'd dreamed about kissing her since he'd glimpsed the fiery woman under the boy's clothes and tattered cap. His conscience berated him at every turn, beating him into submission. He swore he wouldn't kiss her, but he'd never anticipated her making the first move.

Virginia's eyes drifted closed as her lips touched his. With both hands, she pulled herself against him. The soft slide of her mouth against his made him unravel. His arms instinctively closed around her, pulling her against him as his hands roamed her satin clad curves.

Although the kiss began a tender exploration, it demanded more. She clung to him as if she both needed and provided his salvation. Her inquisitive fingers slid through his hair.

He darted his tongue across her lips, tasting her. She gasped, and he seized the moment by deepening the kiss. Her grip tightened, and she returned it with fervor.

Holding her in his arms had been amazing, but kissing

her, tasting her, drove him to the breaking point. He wanted to protect her, help her find her way. Never had he wanted to take advantage of her. If he didn't stop the madness, it would consume them both. He refused to break her heart...or have his broken again.

But where his head argued with him, his body raged against all rational thought. Without breaking the kiss, he backed her to the chaise and pulled her into his lap as he sat down. Her silken skirts inched up, revealing a stocking-clad knee. He fingered the hem of the gown as he kissed her, drawing lazy circles with his fingertips on her thighs.

She moaned against his mouth.

He pulled back. Her breathing was heavy, her eyes dark with need. He stilled but held her, afraid if he spoke, if he breathed, she would get up and walk out the door. If he didn't control himself, he would ruin her. But if he denied the chemistry between them, she would leave, finding someone else to sate the desire now coursing through her. Nathaniel feared that either way, he would never be able to forgive himself for her fate. *Damned if you do...*

CHAPTER SEVEN

"Nathaniel," Ginny whispered, afraid to break the spell between them. Her heart raced. The heat of his body seeped into her as his grip tightened.

She'd dreamed of kissing him, but her imagination had failed her. No one had ever dared kiss her in such a way. All passion and desperation. Her gaze lingered on his mouth. His breath mixed with hers as she gently massaged his scalp, loving the way his hair slid through her fingers like a mountain spring.

"You shouldn't have kissed me," he replied, his voice barely audible.

"Why not?" Ginny shifted in his lap, bringing her body closer to his, her lips hovering above his own.

His eyes drifted closed. "Because, I...we shouldn't be doing this."

"Do you not want my attentions?" she asked, purposely teasing him with the same question he'd posed moments before.

He opened his eyes and groaned as she slid her hand down to cup his face. "I want them more than I've ever wanted anything in my life." His confession sent a surge of pride through her.

She stroked his lower lip with her fingertip. "Then why do you seem hesitant?"

He caught her wrist, his eyes flashing with warning. "Your safety is my responsibility. I'm supposed to be taking care of you, not taking advantage of you."

"I'm not a child, Nathaniel." She leaned back and pulled her hand from his grip. "Besides, if I remember correctly, I kissed you."

Nathaniel put his hands on her hips and tried to push her from his lap. "I should have stopped you."

She dug her fingers into his shoulders and clung to him. "Stopped me?"

He sighed when she refused to budge. "Yes, I should have stopped you, but I didn't. I took advantage of your innocent kiss."

"Innocent?" Ginny stared at him. "I may never have kissed a man like that before, but I can assure you, my innocence is no concern of yours."

"You're playing a dangerous game, Virginia." His voice dropped an octave as his hands slid down to cup her backside and drag her against him.

Her gown slid up, and she felt the press of his arousal against the sensitive area between her thighs. A surge of need and desperation clawed at her. She wanted him to kiss her again, to show her what these rioting emotions and sensations meant.

"I need you, Nathaniel," she said, unsure exactly what she really, truly needed from him. She knew about sex. She'd just spent the last three days in a brothel thanks to him. But never in her life had that curiosity flared to life the way it did when he touched her.

He shook his head. "You don't know what you need."

"Then tell me," she begged rocking her body against him.

Nathaniel groaned. His hands slid up to her neck. His fingers tangled in her hair. "Stop tormenting me." He leaned his forehead against hers. His lips hovered above hers.

"Shut up and kiss me again."

She captured his lips, holding them captive with her own. Her arms wrapped around his neck and she poured the entirety of herself into the kiss, hoping he would open for her, accept her, love her.

Their mingled moans filled the room as the kiss stretched into what felt like an endless parade of sensations. He kissed the corner of her mouth then her jaw, exploring the length of her neck with his lips and tongue.

Ginny clung to him. "Nathaniel, please, touch me." She ground her hips against him, her chest brushing against his.

His hand dropped to her thigh, sliding between the fabric and her skin. She gasped as his fingers brushed the edge of her panties. Ginny granted his silent request by rising up on her knees. When his finger brushed her center, she whimpered, burying her face against his shoulder.

"Quiet, love. If you need to cry out, kiss me." He slid his finger into her.

"Oh sweet mercy." She moaned as he stroked and caressed her. "Nathaniel..." Her voice drifted off as his thumb found a sensitive spot hidden between her thighs.

"Does that feel good?" he whispered against her ear.

"Y-yes," she stuttered. Her body rocked against his hand, finding a rhythm to compliment his movements. A blaze of need flared to life, and Ginny struggled to break free before it consumed her.

"Don't fight it." He added a second finger, stretching her, stroking faster and harder.

Ginny threw her head back and let the sensations consume her, her breaths coming in short bursts, her body hurtling toward the unknown at full speed.

"That's it, Virginia, sing for me." He kissed her throat.

As if a dam broke inside her mind, Ginny embraced the pulsing intense pleasure starting in the pit of her stomach and radiating to her tips of her fingers and toes. Nathaniel pulled her close and kissed her to silence her cries of pleasure. After what seemed like an eternity, she collapsed against him, weakened from...whatever that was.

He removed his hand from beneath her skirt and pulled a handkerchief from his pocket. After he cleaned himself, he tucked the cloth back in his vest and stroked her bare shoulder. "Was that what you needed?" he asked.

She smiled. "Maybe." Ginny sat up and kissed him. "What do you need?"

"You." He pulled her into his embrace and kissed her forehead.

"Good answer."

"Let's go home." He helped her to her feet and then stood, straightening his suit and handing her the discarded shawl. "There's a mirror in the corner, fix yourself. You look completely ruined."

Ginny snorted. "Ruined? What century are you in?"

"The twentieth, and I'm still a gentleman at heart. I don't believe in showcasing my dalliances."

She glanced in the mirror and sighed. Ginny rearranged her hair, fixing a curl into place again. "Is that all I am? A dalliance?"

Nathaniel stepped up behind her and placed his hands on her shoulders. "No, I was just making a point. I prefer to keep what happens between us...between us."

Ginny met his gaze in the mirror. "All right."

He dropped his hands and offered his arm. "Shall we?"

When she linked her arm through his, Ginny took a deep breath and grinned at him, feeling a bit wicked over what had transpired just moments before. She couldn't help but tease him. "Do I look ravished?"

Nathaniel's gaze snapped to hers. "Ravishing, yes. Not ravished...not yet." He winked.

They stepped through the office door and into the bustle and commotion of the club. There were easily twice as many people milling about, drinking and dancing. Ginny kept a tight grip on Nathaniel as they wove through the crowd.

Some of the guests stopped her to compliment her voice and offer to buy her a drink. Nathaniel politely declined for her. Beside him, she felt confident and safe. After all he'd done for her, Ginny knew deep down that Nathaniel would never hurt her. He was a protector by nature. Once they exited the townhouse, Ginny took a deep breath and glanced at her escort.

He slid his hand in hers, entwining their fingers. "Come on."

They walked a few paces to the next home and up the small staircase leading to the back door. Nathaniel knocked on the door twice and waited.

A slender man in a suit opened the door. "Good evening, sir." The man stepped aside, allowing them entry.

"Good evening, Basset." Nathaniel nodded and gestured toward Ginny. "This is Miss Chapman. She'll be staying with us."

"Very well, sir." Basset led them into a large foyer with a staircase.

"That will be all, Basset. Thank you."

The butler turned and disappeared, leaving Ginny to gawk at the exquisite, yet tastefully masculine décor.

"This is your home?" she asked as she ran her hand over the mahogany banister.

"One of them." Nathaniel watched her as he leaned against the wall.

Ginny turned toward him her eyes wide as if she just realized something. "Where are the others?"

"I have one in London, one in New Orleans, another in Saint Louis, and this townhouse," he replied with an almost hesitant expression.

"Do you own clubs in all those cities?" Ginny studied him.

"No, just Baton Rouge."

"How can you afford so many homes? Not to mention the car outside?" How had she not questioned his wealth before? At first it was a welcomed luxury, but a pit of dread settled in her stomach.

"I was granted part of my inheritance before I left England to start a business in America." He gestured toward the stairs. "Shall we?"

Ginny ascended the staircase ahead of him. She turned into the first room at the top. Nathaniel followed her, flicking the light on and illuminating a luxurious bedroom with dark blue curtains and bedding.

She spun around to face him. "The club, right? Your business you started."

"Yes, I started the club, but prohibition and then the economy's crash caused a lot of problems. My business nearly collapsed under the weight of the ban of alcohol. Levi helped me establish a willing, and reliable, network of suppliers."

"Moonshine?" Ginny asked as all the pieces fell together in her mind as he nodded. "That's why you were at our farm, buying moonshine?"

Nathaniel sighed and rubbed the back of his neck. "It's a bit more complicated than that."

"How?" she asked, crossing her arms.

"I've been buying shine from your father since 1922."

"1922?" Ginny sat down hard on the settee at the foot of the bed and struggled to wrap her mind around the implications of Nathaniel's words. "The day I met you, I found my father's still. I hadn't even known he was making shine until that moment."

Nathaniel knelt in front of her.

"You." She pushed her hand against his chest to keep him away. "You're the reason they came to my house."

He took her hand and held it against his chest, his heart beating beneath her touch. She saw the regret in his eyes before he even opened his mouth.

"No, no, you brought this on me. All of this." She jerked her hand away and pushed off the settee. The room suddenly felt too small. She wanted to leave. "I demand you take me home. Now."

Nathaniel had risen to his feet, standing between her and the door. "You can't go home, Virginia. Not yet."

"Why?" she screamed, tears welling up in her eyes. "You

claim you're protecting me, yet all you've done is keep me prisoner." She pointed an accusing finger at him. "You came to talk to my father that day. Did you argue with him? Threaten him? Did you send those men to kill my family?"

"I did no such thing, Virginia." Nathaniel dropped his hands to his sides and shrugged. "Deep down you know I'm telling you the truth." He took a step closer with his hand outstretched.

"Don't touch me." She retreated until her back hit the wall.

"Fine." He held his hands up in surrender, keeping his voice calm. "Virginia, I had nothing to do with those men. I would have protected your family if I had even known they were planning on confronting your father."

"Then why do you insist on keeping me prisoner? Let me go home." She choked on a sob.

"I can't. They might return and right now..." He paused, balling his hands into fists. "Your family isn't there, Virginia."

She collapsed to the floor. "What do you mean?" The tears streamed freely down her face. "Are they dead?"

Nathaniel ran his hand through his hair looking as though he'd rather be surrounded by a pit of vipers than facing her.

"I had a man return to Alton while we were on the river. My lawyer in Saint Louis contacted me as soon as we docked. Four of your brothers are safe and I've ensured they're well taken care of until I can return north. Two of them are still missing. Your father, however..." He glanced away.

Ginny's world shattered.

"He's dead," she whispered.

The dam of emotion she'd held contained for the last week and a half burst from deep inside of her. She wailed, her body heaving with the force of emotion. She felt her heart break with the confirmation of her worst fears.

She barely registered when Nathaniel knelt beside her and pulled her against his chest. As much as she wanted to fight him, to beat her fists against his chest and scream profanities in his face, Ginny craved the comfort.

He sat down and pulled her into his lap, rocking her against his broad chest. "I'm sorry, Virginia. Truly I am. I would have protected him if I had known..."

Silence descended on them, and after what felt like an eternity, Ginny pushed away and climbed from his embrace. She turned her back to him and stared at the mirror next to the door. Her artistically applied makeup smeared across her red swollen eyes, making her look more like a raccoon than a woman.

"Get out," she demanded without turning to face Nathaniel.

"Virginia." He came up behind her. When he put his hand on her shoulder, she shrugged his touch off.

"You brought this on me...on my family." She met his gaze in the mirror. "You killed my father."

He stiffened behind her, the pain in his expression quickly disappearing, giving way to a look of indifference.

"Yes, your father's fate was unfortunate, but remember, it was my money that sustained you for the last ten years. Without me, your entire family would be standing in the breadlines without a roof over your head. Your father made the decision that the risk was worth the reward."

Before she could reply, Nathaniel turned and walked out of the room. Ginny heard the click of the key as it turned in the tumbler, effectively locking her inside a gilded cage.

"I hate you, Nathaniel Blackthorne!" Ginny screamed as she picked up a vase of freshly cut flowers and hurled it at the locked door. The shattered remnants scattered around her feet, mingling with the pieces of her broken heart.

Throwing the door open, Nathaniel stormed into the

spare bedroom. He loosened his tie and pulled the jacket off, tossing it onto the bed.

"What in the hell just happened?" he asked the empty room.

A mass of fury, confusion, and frustration balled in the pit of his stomach. He'd been blinded by her beauty, her performance, her unabashed pleasure. Nathaniel growled in frustration. He knew it would only be a matter of time before she discovered the ugly truth...all of it. He sighed and continued to strip, throwing all his clothes on a pile.

He reached over and rang the bell. He'd dismissed Basset for the evening he remembered with regret. No matter, his servant would come regardless. A twinge of guilt assailed him. It seemed as though all his promises were empty lately.

A knock at the door a few moments later drew his attention from the concerns flitting around in his mind. He opened the door.

"You rang, sir?" Basset stood before him, the perfect picture of a dutiful servant.

"Yes, come in." He ushered Basset into the room and closed the door.

"I fear I've made quite a mess of things, Basset. Miss Virginia will be commandeering my chambers it seems. I've locked the door, for her own safety." He withdrew the key from his trouser pocket. "Please make sure she remains confined to the room until I return tomorrow evening."

"Yes, sir."

"Make sure to supply her with whatever she requests, within reason, mind you." Nathaniel sighed. "Just remember, she is not to leave that room."

Basset nodded. "As you wish, sir. Will that be all?"

Nathaniel nodded. "I believe so. Thank you."

His servant left the room, leaving him alone with his thoughts.

"You've fucked things up again," he muttered to himself. He trudged into the bathroom and turned on the hot water.

As the bath filled, Nathaniel stripped completely. He slipped into the water as it continued to fill.

The heat bit into his flesh, stinging and then warming him to the core. He leaned his head back against the porcelain rim of the tub. Once the water nearly submersed him, he turned it off and relaxed in the scalding liquid.

Images flashed through his mind. Virginia descending the stairs at Pamela's. Watching her take the stage at Casa de Luna, the stage lighting making her glow. The pink flush as her climax consumed her as she straddled him in his office. Even an hour later, her scent lingered in his mind, the taste of her on his lips. He'd promised to leave her alone, to leave her untouched.

But she'd kissed him and his resolve shattered...just like she had with pleasure, then with pain. He shook his head, knowing he'd been a fool to keep her from the truth. Her innocence deserved protection, did it not?

Perhaps in his vain attempt to protect her, he'd forgotten that life doesn't give a shit about one's age or ability to cope with pain and heartache. It certainly hadn't when Sarah had crushed his optimistic youthful spirit.

Nathaniel dipped beneath the surface of the water. The weightless buoyancy levitated his soul for a moment. Then panic crept in. He rose up, causing water to splash everywhere. Wiping a hand across his face, he sputtered and coughed. He shook his head, his hair spraying droplets on the mirror across the room.

"She deserves better." Nathaniel washed himself quickly and rinsed. When he climbed from the tub and wrapped the towel around his waist, he glanced in the mirror. A weary shell of a man stared back at him. "You've nothing to offer her but pain."

Resolution filled him. In the morning, he would call C.R. Evans and make arrangements for Virginia to return to Alton.

CHAPTER EIGHT

A gunshot!

Ginny jumped from the bed, her body thrumming with panic. When another knock echoed in the room, she realized it hadn't been a gunshot.

She climbed from the bed and glanced down. The gown she'd worn the evening before was now wrinkled and tearstained. Ginny frowned and glimpsed in the mirror. Her smeared makeup had dried, making her look like a drowned mummer.

Knock, knock, knock.

She waved a dismissive hand at herself and reached for the door knob. It wouldn't turn. A stab of irritation struck her.

"The bastard locked the door!" she shouted through the wood.

"I merely wished to inquire as to your state of undress, miss. Might I come in?" Basset's familiar voice soothed her ruffled feathers.

"I look like a bedraggled skunk, but I am dressed. Come in, Basset." She backed away from the door as it opened.

He entered the room balancing a tray on one hand. A pair of servants entered behind him carrying a trunk. They set the steamer next to the bed and then left the room, closing the door behind them. Basset placed the covered tray on the desk near the window then turned to her.

"Miss, you do look quite...mussed." He smiled at her, his grey eyes sparkling. "Might I draw you a bath? It would refresh your spirits, I'm sure."

"Where is he, Basset?" Ginny crossed her arms and

refrained from smiling at the kind, older man. She focused on her anger with Nathaniel instead. "Why has he locked me up...again?"

"Perhaps he is concerned with your safety, miss."

She scoffed. "And I'm the Queen of England."

"Is there anything I can do for you, miss?" he asked glancing at her gown.

"I fear I've ruined it." She followed his gaze.

"Nonsense, miss. I'll have it looking like new in no time." He moved to the trunk and opened it. "Here are your other garments. Once you've taken a bath, eaten breakfast, and put on fresh clothes, I'm sure you'll feel right as rain." Basset smiled.

Her anger dissipated at his kindness, but a burning question still nagged at her. "Where is Nathaniel, Basset?"

"He informed me that he would return this evening to fetch you."

"Fetch me? Am I now his pet?" She planted her hands on her hips and grumbled under her breath. "What time is it?"

"Nearly noon, miss." He walked to the window and drew back the curtain.

The bright sunlight made Ginny blink as she approached the glass. She glanced out the window. A steady stream of traffic, both motorized and pedestrian, lined the streets. Her gaze followed the pavement as it wove deeper into the city. She sighed. The spring flowers blossomed along the avenue as the trees burst with their greens and blooms as well.

Ginny sighed and turned to the friendly servant. "Thank you, Basset."

"If you need anything, miss, just pull this cord." He indicated a ropelike cord hanging from the ceiling along the wall next to the door. "Just lay your gown on the bed; I shall return to fetch it." Basset left her in peace.

Ginny nodded and returned her gaze to the streets below. She pressed her hand to the glass. "If you're out there, Eric, I'll find you."

She moved away from the window and began undressing. Ginny laid the gown on the bed. Her mind wandered back to what Nathaniel had said about her family. *Four of them are safe, two are missing, and Father is dead.* A sudden wave of nausea threatened to double her over. She raced into the bathroom and heaved into the toilet.

Once she regained control of her body, Ginny sat back against the tub. She rested her head against her knees. The silk undergarments provided no barrier between her and the cold porcelain. She shivered and decided to take a bath, hoping it would warm her and provide some form of comfort.

Ginny climbed to her feet and turned on the faucet.

An hour and a good, long soak later, she returned to the bedroom and toweled herself dry. The dress was gone, but a lovely cobalt-blue gown with white lace trimming lay in its place. A pair of silk undergarments lay beside it, as well as a pair of low heeled white shoes. She ran her hand over the dress. *Silk.*

"Nathaniel must have some kind of sick obsession with silk," Ginny mumbled as she picked up the undergarments and pulled them on.

As much as she longed for her trousers and overflowing men's shirts, there was something to be said for the feel of silk against one's skin. No friction, no resistance...all elegance. She sighed as she tugged the dress over her head.

A knock at the door startled her and she dropped the fabric to drape around her ankles before replying. "Come in."

Basset stood in the doorway. "Good afternoon, miss. I've brought someone to help you with your hair and makeup." He stepped aside, revealing Pamela.

She swept into the room with a large bag hanging from her arm.

"Hello, sugar." Her gaze filtered down over the gown and then back up to Ginny's face.

"Pamela, what are you doing here?" Ginny asked as Basset took his leave and closed the door.

"I should ask you the same question, darlin'." Her dark eyes drifted to the bed and then back to Ginny.

"What do you mean?" Ginny shook her head in confusion.

"This is Nathaniel's bedroom, and that is his bed." She set the bag down on the settee. "I see he wasted no time in claiming you. It's lovely to see I haven't lost my touch for seduction."

"Seduction? What are you talking about?" Ginny glanced at the bed as the realization washed over her like a bucket of leeches being dumped over her head. "He didn't...well...I mean..."

"There's no need to be embarrassed, sugar. I just pray he does right by you after..."

"After what?" Ginny thrust her hands on her hips.

"After you two made love." Pamela grinned at Ginny's obvious discomfort with the conversation. "Well I assume it was making love in your case, can't see as he would treat you like a common whore." She tapped her fingers against her lips. "Although, come to think of it, it's been a long while since I've seen Nathaniel show a girl this much attention. I mean well, first the transformation, and now the seduction."

"We didn't have sex," Ginny snapped. "He kissed me and well...some other things happened, but there was most definitely no 'making love' last night." She threw herself down on the settee. "I hate him."

Pamela sat down next to her, moving the bag to the floor. "What happened?"

"You knew what he was, and yet you left me with him...you let him take me."

"If by 'what he was' you mean a savvy businessman who sells illegal liquor and has more influence than the governor of our fair state, then yes, darlin', I know who he is." Pamela wrapped her arm around Ginny. "He's done some things he's not proud of, and he's a dangerous man. But don't think for one second that Nathaniel Blackthorne would let harm come to you."

"He's the reason my father is dead."

"Do you really believe that?" Pamela asked, brushing Ginny's damp hair back from her face. "I've known him since he first came to America, and if there's one thing I'd stake my life on, it's his admiration for loyalty." She sighed. "He always takes care of those who are loyal to him. Always."

Ginny sat in silence, mulling over Pamela's words. Her fingers twisted in the lace edging her cobalt blue silk skirt.

"Now, let's get you ready." Pamela reached down for her bag.

"Ready for what?" Ginny asked in surprise.

"Nathaniel has requested your presence this evening at the club. I think he's in hopes of you singing again."

"I won't do it." Ginny stood and crossed to the window. How dare he assume she would put herself on stage again after his confession.

"You've become the talk of the town, sugar. One song and the whole of Baton Rouge is talking about the Nightingale of New Orleans." She winked. "Clever marketing on Nathaniel's part. He serves only the best clientele in the state, as do I. Your little number last night has the town atwitter."

"It was just a song." Ginny felt the heat rising in her cheeks. "It wasn't anything special."

"While I admire your humility, darlin', it sounds like your voice is much more special than even you realize." As Pamela searched the bag, she nodded to the settee beside her. "Sit down and let me get you ready for your encore."

"I can't do this, Pamela. I won't do it. Not for him." She returned to the settee and sat down, facing Pamela.

"Then don't do it for him. Do it for you." Pamela pinned Ginny's hair up and began applying foundation. "Sing your heart out. Take this moment and make it yours."

Ginny sat silent as Pamela applied the makeup and added the finishing touches on her lipstick before moving onto her hair. As she styled it, Ginny felt a sense of calm and resolution settle on her. She would sing.   Not for Nathaniel, but for her father, who always said she sounded like an angel sent straight from heaven. She would make her daddy proud.

"Will you be there?" she asked meeting Pamela's dark eyes.

"You bet, sugar." Pamela grinned. "I wouldn't miss this for the world."

Nathaniel glanced at his watch and then tucked it into his vest pocket. They were late. He frowned as the door opened revealing a couple instead of Virginia and Pamela.

"They'll be here, boss." Thomas came up beside him as if sensing his anxiety.

"They should have been here twenty minutes ago. It's not like they have to cross town, for God's sake." Nathaniel straightened his cuffs and rebuttoned his jacket.

Thomas nodded before returning to his duties behind the bar.

The club had twice as many patrons as it had the night before. While normally Nathaniel would take this as a sign of good fortune, he worried about Virginia's reaction to his request. She'd only promised to sing one song, one night. But they'd fallen in love with his little songbird.

Nathaniel shook his head. Since when did she become *his*? He cleared his throat and picked up the glass of water Thomas had left for him. The cool liquid refreshed him.

He'd spent the morning trying to formulate a plan to reunite Virginia with her family. As much as he wanted her to be his indefinitely, he'd shattered her family with one careless act. He should never have gone to her family's farm, not himself. It had been the main reason for having Earl and Levi serve as his liaisons to his suppliers. Those rival gangs thirsted for his business. They wanted to crush him, make him suffer for his success. Unfortunately, Mr. Chapman had paid the price.

He couldn't fix it. Couldn't undo the damage he'd caused to her family. But he could repay them for their loyalty...and their sacrifice.

Thomas cleared his throat and motioned toward the entrance. "She's here."

When he looked up, Nathaniel saw Pamela coming through the door. Behind her was Virginia, clad in vibrant blue and white, looking like a goddamned angel and tempting him to sin like the devil. He set his glass down and crossed the room.

"Good evening, Pamela...Virginia." He bowed to them and offered his arms to both ladies. "Allow me to show you to your seats."

Pamela took his arm without hesitation, flashing him a brilliant smile. Virginia however, glared at him before resting her hand on his arm.

"You both look lovely this evening." He turned to Virginia and whispered in her ear, "Thank you for coming."

Virginia shivered, and a curl tumbled from its mooring. He wanted to brush it to the side and press a kiss to her neck where it rested against her pale skin. Before he could act on it, she tucked it back with her free hand.

Disappointment crushed his longing. It was soon replaced by self-control. He had promised himself he wouldn't touch her—not again—lest he prove unable to refrain from possessing her completely. Nathaniel glanced at her out of the corner of his eye. Oh, a mighty battle warred inside of him, for she tempted him something fierce.

They reached a small table toward the front of the room, next to the stage. He held the chairs out for both ladies, and once they were seated, he sat across from them.

Pamela smiled at him, her neat, white, feline smile complimented by her dark hair and the crimson of her gown.

She leaned forward, showing a hint of cleavage.

"Is that the governor?" she whispered, conspiratorially gesturing over her shoulder at the couple seated two tables to the left, near the wall.

Nathaniel nodded. "Yes, and the mayor is here as well with his wife and sister-in-law."

Pamela smiled in appreciation and waved her hand toward Virginia. "Looks like you've captured the attention of the elite, sugar. What are you going to sing tonight?"

"I have a song in mind, but I'm not sure if it's appropriate or not."

"As long as it's not an Irish shanty or a vulgar riverboat jig, I'm sure it will be fine." Pamela rested her hand on Virginia's.

Nathaniel felt a surge of protective jealousy ricochet through him. He wished it were him offering her comfort and encouragement. When Virginia's gaze snapped up to meet his, her eyes narrowed and her pouty red lips thinned. No, it would seem she hadn't forgiven him, not that he'd expected he to do so. She had every right to hate him.

The band played a lovely swaying jazz melody. That's when a young man approached the table, his gaze fixed on Virginia. Nathaniel had to bite back the snarl that wanted to escape from his lips.

"May I have this dance?" he asked Virginia, offering his hand.

"Absolutely." She smiled at the gentleman, completely avoiding eye contact with Nathaniel.

He whisked her to the dance floor where they joined several other couples as the sweet music played.

"Would you like to dance, Nathaniel?" Pamela asked, her voice like smoke on the bayou, dark and sensual with a hint of a threat.

"Of course," Nathaniel replied, offering his hand to her.

As he led Pamela to the dance floor, his gaze unconsciously strayed to Virginia. His heart clenched at the sight of her smiling at the handsome young man who held her in his arms.

"Stop scowling," Pamela whispered as he pulled her into his embrace. Their feet followed the motions, but their minds were obviously bent on something else.

Nathaniel didn't respond. He didn't know how to respond. How could he have anticipated the events of the last two weeks? He'd never imagined the pint-sized river rat becoming more to him than an obligation of loyalty. But somehow, even though he refused to admit it to himself, she'd weaseled her way into his heart.

"Look at me, Nathaniel Blackthorne." Pamela's voice broke through the haze of thoughts.

He met her dark, unwavering gaze.

"I know you better than most...almost as well as I know Levi." She paused and took a steadying breath. "I've never seen you act in such a way."

"She's my responsibility. Because of me she's homeless and fatherless." He glanced beyond Pamela to see Virginia laughing breathlessly in a stranger's embrace.

"You can't play me for a fool, Nathaniel. You might think that it's your actions that led to her family's fate, but the only thing that matters is that you were there for her when she needed someone to care." Pamela watched him intently, a smirk tugging at the corners of her lips. "Deny it all you want, but you love that girl."

Nathaniel scoffed.

"She's not Sarah." Pamela reached up to cup his chin in her hand, forcing him to meet her gaze. "Virginia is innocent, so don't you dare treat her as anything other than that."

"Do you honestly think so little of me, Pamela?" he asked as the twist of guilt lodged in his chest.

"I know I found her in your bedroom this afternoon, and although she swears you two didn't have sex, I could see the desire in her eyes. If you sleep with her, then you'd best be ready to make an honest woman of her." Pamela sighed.

"She's not like me...not like my girls. Virginia deserves better, and I'm not sure whether that includes you or not."

"What are you trying to say?" He arched a brow. Pamela was not often this forthcoming when it came to his personal business. They were business partners and had been friends a long time, but she'd never made it a point to state her opinion on his personal affairs.

"You're a good man, Nathaniel. Savvy as well as ingenious, charming and loyal to a fault, but you're caught up in a dangerous game. We all are. Virginia has no stake in this, no understanding of how it works. If you choose to bed her and then break her heart, I will cut off your cock myself and hang it on the wall above my fireplace." Her gaze narrowed.

"Ouch." He cringed. Her threat lingered between them for a moment before he continued. "I have no intention of hurting her. I've only ever wanted to keep her safe."

"Good."

"I'm returning her to Alton next week," he added, remembering his conversation with C.R. Evans earlier that day.

Pamela's eyes grew wide with surprise before she arched a brow. "Does Virginia know about your plan?"

"No," Nathaniel replied. The music stopped, forcing them to cease their dance and join in the applause.

As they returned to their seats, Pamela leaned close to him. "I suggest you fix whatever ill will is between you two. And remember what I told you." She jabbed him in the ribs, digging her nail into the fabric of his vest.

The young man returned Virginia and she thanked him with a whimsical smile. Nathaniel refrained from the sudden urge to hit the youth. Virginia turned her attention to Pamela when the young man left. The two women chatted under their breath before he could take it no longer.

"I'll have Thomas announce you." He stood. "If you'll excuse me, I have some business matters to attend." Without waiting for a reply, he walked toward his office.

As he reached the bar, he called Thomas over.

"Yes, boss?" He smoothed his mustache, twirling the end into a curl.

"I need you to introduce Virginia. I have some things I have to take care of." He knocked on the bar with his knuckles. "Don't let her leave with anyone except Pamela, and remember, no alcohol for her. I'll be back in an hour or two."

Nathaniel went into his office, grabbed a thick envelope from the locked top drawer, and then returned to the boisterous club.

"Ladies and gentlemen, it is my pleasure to welcome back the Nightingale of New Orleans." Thomas' voice boomed through the crowded house.

Nathaniel made his way to the door. When he reached Carl, he nodded to the man, but his softened gaze was fixated on the stage. He sighed. Not Carl too. It seemed they'd all been captivated by the little river rat. *She's not so little and looks nothing like that tomboy who ran into me on the docks.*

The soft strains of her voice filled the stagnant air, as if the room held its collective breath waiting for her to sing.

Nathaniel turned slowly. When he saw her, his breath ceased, his heart doubling in rhythm.

The way the light hit her hair and illuminated her gown. She looked like an ethereal goddess, gracing the world with her presence and her golden voice. Her eyes met his across the crowd. And for a moment, the world disappeared. They stared at each other as she continued to sing. Her voice for him alone as if they were the only people left on the face of the Earth.

Nathaniel turned away and stepped out the door into the darkened stairwell. His heart pounded and his head ached. His dry mouth begged for something strong to wash away the memory of her taste. But he knew, beyond a doubt, he would never find another woman like his songbird.

CHAPTER NINE

The car rumbled to a stop just behind the building nestled next to the dock. He stepped out into the humid night air and inhaled. As he walked around to the dock, he found the *Mississippi Queen* tied next to *The Sentinel*, who was flanked on the opposite side by the *Blue Moon*.

Nathaniel grinned. At least Levi had returned. He strode up the gangplank and climbed aboard the *Mississippi Queen*.

"Levi," he shouted down the corridor of the ship.

"What are you doing here, Blackthorne?" Levi asked behind him.

He turned. "There you are. Any problems?"

Levi leaned against the door frame and pulled a handkerchief from his pocket. "None." He cocked his head. "Why aren't you at the club?"

Nathaniel straightened. "I wanted to be here when you returned. I'll take a case of the rum with me. You can have the boys deliver the rest tomorrow evening."

"Go ahead." Levi nodded and pointed to a room down the hall. "Care to tell me the real reason you're here and not carousing with the elites at the club?"

He hefted a case in his arms and pushed past Levi. "No."

"How's Virginia?" Levi asked.

Nathaniel paused and attempted to shrug with the case in his arms. "I'll need you to return her to Alton next week." He set the case down on the deck and turned to his friend. "Can I trust you to see that she's returned safely?"

"Why?" Levi crossed his arms.

"Why what?"

"Why are you sending her home? Have you found her brothers? I hope to God you told her about her father."

"I did tell her about her father... She knows everything." He shifted the weight of the case in his arms. "I talked with Evans and he's arranged a home for her in Alton. I've already moved four of her brothers there. The other two are still missing."

"You didn't answer my question."

Nathaniel wanted to scream. "What question?"

"Why are you sending Virginia home?" he asked, his gaze narrowing.

"Because I can't keep her caged up here. She's not mine."

Levi shrugged. "Then make her yours. Some new clothes and a curry comb to tame that mane of hers, and I think she'd be quite the looker."

Nathaniel frowned. He counted it a blessing Levi hadn't seen her transformation thanks to Pamela. "That's beside the point."

"She's pissed at you for what happened, and rightly so. I'd be concerned if she wasn't." Levi rested his hand on Nathaniel's shoulder. "Are you sure this is a good idea? Sending her back into that uncertainty."

"I'll take care of her and her brothers."

"So here or there, she'll still be under your care?" Levi teased.

Nathaniel sighed and scowled at his friend. "I told you—"

"I heard you, 'she's not yours,' but what if she were? Would that be so bad?" Levi shook him. "You're fighting this too much. Take a chance. A girl like her is worth the risk."

"You said the same thing about Sarah."

Levi released him to stroke his beard. "That was eleven years ago, I wasn't quite as observant as I am now. Besides, Virginia is different...in looks, in temperament, in ideals, in motivation...I'd stake my life on it."

A moment of tense silence filled the space between them.

Finally, Levi picked up the case and left Nathaniel standing by the gangplank. He shook his head and darted down to the dock. He caught up to Levi who was closing the rumble seat.

"Come with me." Nathaniel said. "Back to the club."

"I look like hell." He rubbed his hand across his beard.

"We'll stop off at the house and you can clean up. I want to show you something."

"All right, but I hope it's worth it." Levi climbed into the car and Nathaniel followed.

When the duo pulled up to the back door of Nathaniel's townhouse, Levi shook his head. "I'd rather live on my boat."

"Go in and change. Basset will help you find something suitable. Hurry." Nathaniel gestured to the door of his town house.

"You've gotten quite demanding lately," he shot back as he climbed the steps.

Once Levi disappeared into the house, Nathaniel leaned against the car and watched the neighboring home's door. He pulled out his watch. Quarter after ten. Part of him hoped Virginia was still at the club. He'd only been gone for an hour, but he doubted she would linger if he wasn't there demanding she stay.

Fifteen minutes later, the door opened. Nathaniel let out a low whistle. Levi descended the stairs, his navy blue pinstripe suit offset with a white fedora. His beard had been trimmed neatly and his hair slicked back into a fashionable que.

"Speaking of cleaning up nicely." He reached out and straightened Levi's tie. "I haven't seen you this dapper since you last put on your uniform."

Levi slapped his hand away. "What is so goddamn important you made me dress like this?"

Nathaniel gestured to the door. "Let me show you."

Together they entered the house, greeted Nana, and then descended to the basement door. As Carl opened the door, he grinned at them.

"I'm glad you're back, Mr. Blackthorne." Carl nodded as he permitted them entry and closed the door to stand in front of it.

"Has something happened, Carl?" Nathaniel turned his attention to the club.

The band played a lively tune and the couples swirled around on the dance floor. He caught a glimpse of the familiar blue gown in the center of the commotion. Virginia flitted from one dance partner to another.

"Where's Pamela?" he asked. A flash of red caught his eye at the bar.

Pamela stood with her elbows resting on the bar facing the entertainment, a smirk on her lips.

He made his way over to her. "What the hell is going on here? You're supposed to be keeping an eye on her."

"That's what I'm doing. They're only dancing, Nathaniel. No one has stolen away your precious songbird." Pamela glared at him, then her gaze slipped over his shoulder and softened for a moment before turning to ice. "What's he doing here?"

Levi bristled. "I was wondering the same thing. What, not enough men to keep you busy tonight, Pamela?"

"Sticks and stones, river rat," she hissed.

"Enough, both of you," Nathaniel snapped as he searched for Virginia in the crowd. Once he caught sight of her, he remained focused as he contemplated what to do next. He didn't want to cause a scene. That would just draw attention to them.

Levi followed his gaze. "Nathaniel, is that Virginia?"

Nathaniel nodded.

"Holy hell, I guess I was a bit off. I knew she'd clean up well, but this..." He whistled low, his voice trailing off. "She's..."

He turned and glared at his friend. "I'd advise you to swallow the rest of that sentence if you value our friendship."

Levi pinched his mouth closed and raised his hands in

defense. Pamela chuckled, throaty and sensual. As if anything Pamela did could be considered any less than sensual.

"What are you laughing at?" Levi asked turning to the bar.

Nathaniel kept his gaze on Virginia, her radiance obvious to everyone around her. He clenched his hand into a fist and finally turned away.

"This is all his own fault. He asked me to...what was it, Nathaniel? Oh yes, 'make her a lady." Pamela took a sip of her drink, her eyes remaining on Virginia.

"I should have recognized your handiwork," Levi replied holding up a finger to the bartender, one of Thomas' protégés.

"What is that supposed to mean?" Pamela shot him a look.

Nathaniel ignored them as they bantered, even though he remained literally in the middle of their argument. He sighed. These two would forever be at each other's throats. While he understood why, it still irritated him that after eleven years, neither of them would admit the truth to the other. They still denied any attraction existed, even when Nathaniel had asked them separately.

"Don't get your stockings twisted in a knot," Levi replied and took a sip of his drink. "You've always had a way with bringing beauty to the surface. Whether it was art or décor or bedraggled river rats, somehow you see the potential and make it shine."

"Well, Levi, I believe that's the closest thing to a compliment I've received from you in a long time." Pamela glanced at him.

Feeling the attraction between the two of them nearly made Nathaniel want to run into his office and bar the door. Instead he turned to Levi.

"Ask her to dance, for God's sake," he whispered under his breath.

Levi straightened and tossed back the liquor in his glass.

He walked around Nathaniel and offered his hand to Pamela. "Come on, let's cut a rug."

"Ever the gentleman, aren't you, Levi?" Pamela scoffed but placed her gloved hand in his.

Nathaniel exhaled in relief when the two left him alone at the bar. He'd intended to bring Levi as a buffer, a distraction to keep his mind off of Virginia. He'd forgotten his friend's love-hate relationship with Pamela.

His gaze lighted on the pair before drifting to Virginia, who had taken the floor with the governor. He groaned. Had it been wise of him to bring her into this world, into his life? Probably not. But nothing could be done for it. His plan to return her to her family the following week would put him at ease.

Evans had requested a week to prepare the home and make the necessary arrangements for protection. He'd grant him that, but anything more and he knew he'd regret his decision to keep her close. Protection from whom? He scoffed as he picked up the glass Thomas had placed on the bar next to his elbow. He downed the contents and turned to Thomas waiting behind the bar.

"Watch her," he said as he pushed away from the bar and headed for his office.

Once inside, he closed the door, shutting out the noise from the club with near perfect efficiency. He moved to his desk and opened the drawer. Next to his decanter of whisky lay the bottle of shine he'd taken from Virginia the day he'd found her stuffed in his trunk.

He poured a tall glass, knowing it was a bad idea, knowing it would only worsen the guilt and pain. Without hesitation, he drank...and drank...and drank...until the glass was empty and he lay draped in his oversized chair, piss-assed drunk.

The pounding in his head seemed to worsen. Then he realized it wasn't his head. Someone pounded against the door. The sound echoed in his brain and suddenly he wished he hadn't drunk so much. It never boded well when he imbibed alcohol at a quick pace...and moonshine at that. Powerful and quite dangerous stuff.

"Come in," he grumbled, making a half-hearted attempt to sit up.

"Look at you."

He glanced at himself then looked up. Virginia stood before him with her hands on her hips, a scowl marring her fair skin, her lips pursed in agitation. Her twin stood beside her. Wait, were there two of her? He shook his head and grinned at her.

"You're drunk."

"Yes, Virginia, I'm quite foxed, and for good reason." He tried to stand and fell back into the chair. He glanced up at her. "You."

The warm embrace of darkness consumed his consciousness, and he saw her fade as if being absorbed by the shadows of his mind.

Ginny stood staring down at Nathaniel. Was he asleep? She crept closer and poked his shoulder. His head lolled to the side and snored.

"Damn it, Blackthorne," Ginny swore as she turned helplessly. Who could she ask for assistance? The thought of leaving him in his office to sleep it off sounded mighty tempting. She glanced at him.

He'd pulled his tie loose and his hair lay across his forehead, the impeccable part long since destroyed. Even in sleep he looked tense.

The door opened behind her. "Nathaniel." Pamela's voice filtered into the room.

Ginny turned to see Pamela and Levi standing just inside the door. Levi looked about to burst into laughter, his smile smothered behind the back of his hand. Pamela slapped his shoulder.

"Let's get him home." She slipped out of the room and returned with Carl moments later. "Can you carry him home, Carl? I'm not even going to attempt to try to drag him between the three of us."

Ginny said nothing. She watched with her brow furrowed as the events played out in front of her.

Carl nodded and picked Nathaniel up like a sack of grain, hefting him over his shoulder without even a grunt. He carried him through the door.

"Come along, sugar." Pamela gestured with one hand. "Levi and I will escort you back to Nathaniel's home."

Ginny exited the office. The club was empty save for Thomas who cleaned the bar and a few waitresses who were wiping down tables. Thomas waved as she passed and she forced a smile. Her face hurt from smiling. She'd worn a false grin all night, pretending to be amused and entertained by the crowd of people desperate to meet the Nightingale of New Orleans.

She snorted. That title was ridiculous. She'd never even been to New Orleans. Her lessons at the boarding school had come in handy, but she felt like a shiny bauble put on display. Ginny always kept to the shadows, to herself. Being the center of attention exhausted her.

Although she tried to deny it, she'd wanted to make Nathaniel proud of her. Even though every part of her rational mind screamed to beat him senseless for all he'd put her through, Ginny craved his attention. She didn't trust him...hated him, really.

Ginny sighed as they stepped out into the early morning air. The sun wouldn't rise for several hours, but the day was already new and crisp.

Levi slipped past her and opened the door to the townhouse. She stepped inside, followed by Pamela. They moved to the staircase when Ginny turned to them.

"Thank you for your help. I'm sure Basset has Nathaniel taken care of." She nodded stiffly.

Pamela's feline smile betrayed nothing beyond humor at the situation as a whole. "As you wish, sugar." She turned to Levi. "It's been a long time since I've seen the *Blue Moon.*"

A look of shock passed over Levi's face followed by a wicked grin. "Well, I'm sure I can arrange something." He took her arm.

They left Ginny staring after them wondering what kind of history they shared. She shook her head. What did it matter? A question rose in the back of her mind. *Are they lovers?*

Ginny fanned herself with her hand at the thought of Pamela and Levi doing what Nathaniel had done with her the night before. Pushing the curiosity away with both hands, Ginny ascended to the second floor.

Carl appeared at the top of the staircase. "He's in bed now, miss. Just come get me next door if you need any help." He passed her on his way down the stairs.

"Thank you, Carl." She smiled at him.

Basset bustled around the room she'd occupied the night before. He was gathering her belongings and tucking them in the trunk. When he caught sight of her, he bowed.

"My apologies, miss. I'll have your things moved to the other room immediately."

She laid her hand on his arm. "Don't worry about all of that, Basset. They can wait until morning. Go get some rest." Ginny shot him a look of challenge.

He hesitated as if he wanted to protest, but ultimately nodded in agreement. "As you wish, miss. Ring if you need anything."

He moved to the side of the bed where Nathaniel lay unconscious.

"I'll take care of him," she heard herself saying.

"Miss, he's my—"

"I shall take care of him. Go." Ginny nodded to the door.

"Yes, miss." Basset took his leave.

Ginny gathered her nightgown and went into the bathroom to change. Once she'd washed her face, brushed her hair, and pulled on her gown, she returned to find Nathaniel hadn't moved...not an inch.

She noticed Basset had removed Nathaniel's shoes, but he remained fully clothed otherwise. Not caring if she woke him, she began to take off his jacket and vest. Her hand slid against cool metal. She pulled the item from his coat.

A small revolver...a .38 Special if she wasn't mistaken. She'd seen her father's a few times but never touched it. The weight of it in her hand brought the reality of who he was crashing down on her head. *Dangerous.*

She tossed the gun onto the bed next to him and finished pulling off his jacket, followed by his vest. When she reached for the buttons on his shirt, her hands trembled. Two weeks on the riverboat and she'd never seen him without a shirt. Ginny chewed on her lower lip. Perhaps it would be best to leave his shirt and trousers on. He wasn't going to die sleeping in his clothes. Was he?

Her fingertips brushed his skin as she unbuttoned the top few buttons. His warmth infused her and she pulled her hands away as though burned.

"You'll sleep just fine like that," she murmured as she drew the blanket over him.

The soft comforting embrace of the bed called to her. She climbed onto it, sinking into the mattress. When her leg brushed the pistol, she grabbed it and set it on the nightstand beside her pillow before lying down.

Ginny nuzzled against the soft pillow and drew the blanket up over her body. Exhaustion claimed her.

CHAPTER TEN

Warmth called to him. Warmth and silken skin. Nathaniel drew himself closer to the delightful dream, needing the contact. He groaned. A woman in his bed. He liked this dream. It'd been years since he'd brought a woman into his bed. His fingers brushed the silk clad curves and her body arched against him. He cupped her breast, feeling the nipple pebble underneath his thumb and forefinger.

She moaned. "Nathaniel."

He pressed a kiss to her neck and buried his face in the sweet scent of her hair, her skin. Nathaniel never wanted to wake from this dream. He arched his hips, brushing his erection against her backside. The only thing that would make this better is if he pulled the nightgown up and slid inside her.

His fingers closed around the hem of her gown, slowly lifting it over her thighs. She stilled. He continued until his hand brushed her bare hip, his fingertips gliding along the crease of her thigh toward the haven nestled between her legs.

"Nathaniel."

The unmistakable sound of a pistol cocking shattered the dream. The cool press of the barrel against his ribs made his blood freeze. He opened his eyes to find Virginia staring at him, her mouth pressed in a thin line, her nostrils flaring, and fear in her eyes. *Damn.*

"Put the gun down, Virginia." He removed his hands from her person and inched away slowly.

"I never gave you permission to touch me." She

uncocked and lowered the gun but kept it firm in her grip.

"No, and I apologize for that. But you can hardly fault a man for such attention when he finds a woman dressed in only a silk nightgown in his bed."

"You slept next to me on the river boat and never once touched me like that."

His groin tightened thinking about those nights. He hadn't. Not once. But that didn't mean he hadn't wanted to. Even then he'd wanted her with a passion that terrified him.

"Again, I apologize. The shine must have addled my brain. Forgive me."

He pushed away, needing to get out of the bed and away from her lest he do something unforgivable. Nathaniel sat on the edge of the bed, his feet planted firmly on the floor when the room began to spin. He rested his head in his hands and leaned forward, groaning. He barely registered the soft touch on his shoulder.

"Nathaniel, lie down." She pulled his arm.

He collapsed to the side, his head landing on his pillow, and closed his eyes. Forcing himself to take deep breaths, Nathaniel attempted to still the world spinning inside his head.

Her hand stroked his hair. "Would you like some water?" she asked, her voice barely above a whisper.

Nathaniel hazarded a glance at her. She leaned over him, her nightgown hanging off her shoulder leaving a huge expanse of creamy skin exposed to his view. He swallowed and followed the line of the gown where it barely covered her breast. Her nipples pressed against the fabric.

He licked his lips and shook his head. "No, you should just go. I'll be fine with some rest."

"I can't leave you like this." She brushed his hair away from his face. "As much as I want to hate you, I can't stand to see you suffering like this. Even if it is your own stupid fault for drinking too much."

"It's your fault," he croaked.

"You drinking too much is *my* fault?" She scowled.

He wanted to kiss the lines that formed between her eyes. "Yes."

Virginia crossed her arms, emphasizing her breasts. His gaze flicked down for a moment. "You really should put some clothing on." He turned away.

He heard the rustle of the bedding as she shuffled off the bed. When he finally regained control of his body's reaction to her, he glanced over his shoulder.

She pulled on a dressing gown and tied the sash before spinning around to meet his gaze. "Is that better? I'd hate to offend your sensibilities."

"It's not me I'm looking after," he snapped as he made another effort to stand. He grasped the corner of the bedside table to steady himself. "Damn that shine," he grumbled under his breath. "How much did I drink last night?"

"The whole bottle." Virginia crossed the room to pour him a glass of water.

"That would explain the thunderous pain in my skull." He took the proffered glass of water and downed it in one long swallow.

"I'm still angry at you," she said as she refilled the glass in his hand.

"You have every right to be." Nathaniel glanced at her. The sunlight streamed through the window, bringing out the golden streaks in her auburn hair. It lay mussed and tousled against her shoulders. Not nearly as disastrous as the first time he'd seen her.

"Why didn't you tell me the truth while we were on the boat?" she asked, her green eyes bright and fiery.

"About buying moonshine from your father?" Nathaniel shrugged. "I wasn't sure how much your father had told you, and honestly, it didn't concern you." He held up a hand when she opened her mouth. "Although, I should have known when I pulled that bottle of shine from your pocket that you deserved the truth."

"Damn right I did... I still do." She spun away from him.

He grabbed her arm. Her gaze snapped to his, her brow raised in defiant question.

"You're a strong woman. I should have told you the truth as soon as I discovered what had happened to your family," He released her and sighed. "But I didn't want to see your heart break. I couldn't take knowing that I'd caused your family so much trouble...that I'd been the cause of your father's death."

"Nathaniel—"

"Let me apologize." He took a deep breath. "I can't bring your father back, but as I've said before, I always reward those who are loyal to me."

"I don't understand." Virginia scrunched up her nose and shook her head.

"My lawyer is currently making preparations for your brothers. He's found a suitable home for them, and I will provide guards to ensure their safety until I can find the bastards who did this."

"Did you find Matthew and Mark? Please tell me you've found them."

Nathaniel shook his head. "My men haven't located them yet, but they're searching. Your other brothers have already taken residence in the house. I intend to reunite you with them as soon as possible."

Her eyes widened. "You're sending me back to Alton?"

Was that hope bubbling from her?

He steeled himself against the onslaught of unwanted emotion, the selfish need and desire to claim her as his own. *Set her free. She's not yours.* "Yes."

"Is it safe?" she asked.

No, his mind shouted.

"You will be safe once Levi has returned you to your family," he replied, keeping his gut reaction in check.

"Levi?" She stared at him, her lips drawn into a frown. "You're not coming?"

"I have matters here that need my attention. I can't return to Alton for a few months at least."

"So you'll just dump me off at the docks to have me shipped upriver without so much as a..."

Nathaniel glared at her. "As a what?"

"A discussion," she replied through clenched teeth. "What if I don't want to go without you?"

"You don't have a choice." He stalked toward the door.

Virginia's hand grasped the back of his shirt. He spun around to face her and regretted it the moment their eyes met. Her wild hair, the silk peeking through the dressing gown, her luscious lower lip pressed into a pout as she clutched his shirt, it all became too much. If he were less of a man, he'd ravish her without a thought to her future.

"Release me," he growled.

"Or what? You'll spank me, lock me in this room, deprive me of my supper!" she mocked him. "I'm not a child!"

"I'm well aware of that." He wrenched himself from her grip.

"Then stop treating me like I don't have a mind of my own." She stepped closer, her gaze fierce and glinting with mischief.

"Virginia." He attempted to keep his tone stern, but her proximity proved to be disconcerting. Nathaniel's back hit the door as he tried to escape her. He stared down at the petite woman who held him enthralled.

"Do you not believe a woman can know her own mind...her own desires?"

"I won't take advantage of your situation." Nathaniel refused to budge.

"Are you speaking of your intention to return me to my family post haste?" Her fingers began to work the buttons free from their tiny nooses, exposing his chest as his shirt fell open. "Or what happened this morning before I put a gun to your ribs?"

"Virginia, I have no intention of seducing you. My duty is to protect you and return you to the safety of your family." Nathaniel closed his eyes as she unfastened the last button and her fingertips trailed across his bare stomach, tracing the top of his trousers.

"There's a flaw to your plan, Nathaniel." She leaned forward and pressed a kiss to the center of his chest.

Oh sweet glorious fucking mercy. "Virginia, stop."

"You never asked me what I wanted." She slid her arms beneath his shirt wrapping them around his bare waist. Her eyes upturned. He felt her gaze searching his face.

"What do you want from me, Virginia?" he asked, his voice breathless, his heart racing. It took all of his control to not pull her against him, capture her lips, and carry her the five paces to bed.

"I want you, Nathaniel." She slid her hands down over his ass. "I want you to kiss me again, like you did that night at the club. I want you to make me a woman in truth. Make me yours."

"You don't know what you're asking." He groaned as she pressed closer to him, rubbing her stomach against his arousal.

"I know exactly what I'm asking for. I'm asking for you to make love to me in that bed." She batted her lashes at him.

"That wouldn't change anything, Virginia. You're still getting on that ship to return to Alton without me." He ground his teeth together. Her sweet scent teased him, the heat of her body drew him like a moth to the flame. Nathaniel applauded his threadbare self-control.

"We'll see about that." She brought her hand to rest on the fastening of his trousers.

"Virginia..." He tried to scold her, to tell her the truth, but when her warm hand caressed his cock, he jerked and all coherent thought flew out into the Louisiana morning air.

"So soft, Nathaniel, and yet so hard." Virginia grinned up at him. "Let me see it."

He freed himself from the confines of the fabric. When both her hands enclosed him, he growled. "Virginia."

He snatched her by the arms and pushed her back until she fell on the bed. She caught herself and watched wide eyed as he pulled his shirt off and shucked his trousers. When he prowled closer, she backed up on the bed.

"You're overdressed." He pulled the sash holding her dressing gown.

She slid it over her shoulders. Her silk nightgown left little to the imagination, yet he craved an uninhibited view of her body. Grasping the hem, he drew it up, his hands gliding over her thighs.

"Nathaniel," she whimpered as he pulled it out from underneath her bum, exposing her to his gaze. When he drew it over her head and tossed it onto the floor, she covered herself with her hands, falling back onto the bed.

"No, you asked for this. I deserve to see all of you so I can commit every curve, every inch of you to memory." He drew her legs apart and settled between her thighs. His gaze drifted over the soft triangle of hair. Nathaniel ran his hands along the inside of her thighs. When he brought his head down to taste her, she gasped.

"What are you doing?" she asked, trying to back away from him.

He hooked his arms around her thighs and pressed a kiss to her sex. "Tasting you." Nathaniel flicked his tongue across her, savoring her sweet flavor.

Virginia groaned and raked her hands through his hair, trying to draw him away. He licked her again.

"Nathaniel, stop! Please." She whimpered, her breathing sharp and pronounced.

He pulled away, sitting back and watching her.

She lay splayed against his bed, her hair a halo of golden auburn, her lips parted, her skin flushed a delightful hue of pink. She stared at him, blinking, her index finger between her teeth.

Nathaniel arched a brow. "I warned you not to play this game."

Virginia sat up slowly, bringing herself onto her knees in front of him. She wrapped her arms around his neck and kissed him. The gentle press of her lips became a carnal exploration as he locked his arms around her and opened his mouth to deepen the kiss.

His hands grasped her hips, his fingers brushing the curve of her ass and the crease where her backside met her legs. She trembled in his arms. He broke the kiss.

"This is your last chance," he murmured against her lips. "Tell me to stop."

Her fingers slid into his hair, the touch oddly calming. "Take all of me."

Ginny wondered what had happened to her hesitation, to her anger. She'd woken in his arms, his hands on her breasts, his arousal pressed to her ass. Self-preservation had reared its head and she'd pulled the gun from the dresser.

But that was before. Ginny licked her lips and dove into madness.

Nathaniel's naked body pressed against hers, the feel of his heat and strength seeping into her. She craved more contact, more sensation, more everything. Her hands slid into his silky hair as she arched against him. He pressed a kiss to her throat as he lay her back onto the blankets and settled between her thighs.

His erection pressed to her folds. She bit her bottom lip in anticipation. He paused as he positioned himself at her entrance.

"Are you sure?" he asked, his voice soft as his breath as it brushed her lips.

Ginny nodded before pulling his head down so their lips

met. When he slid into her, she whimpered and arched into him. He filled her, stretching and moving. Her grip tightened, her fingernails digging into his skin. With a thrust, he seated himself and kissed her deeply.

Her gasp lost in the kiss, she moved against him as if trying to find a stable point in the onslaught of sensations. The gentle rock of his hips brought a warmth from deep within. She held onto him, finding a fixed point in her topsy-turvy world.

The familiar sensations infiltrated her mind and body. The same ones she'd experienced the night at the club when he'd brought her pleasure. She wrapped her legs around his waist and let him guide her.

He peppered kisses along her jaw as he made love to her, their bodies gliding together in unison. She gasped as the pleasure built deep pushing her higher and higher. When he shifted his hips to grind against hers, she shattered. Pleasure sparked through her like heat lightning against a midnight sky.

Ginny screamed his name, her voice echoing off the walls. The cries of pleasure became whimpers of bliss as the sensations of her climax subsided.

Nathaniel thrust into her again and then pulled back with a groan, spending himself on her stomach. He leaned his head against her shoulder, pressing a kiss to her damp skin. It seared her like a brand.

Ginny ran her hands through his hair. "Thank you," she whispered.

He pulled back and looked down at her, his mussed hair falling across his mismatched, handsome eyes. "For what?"

"For giving me what I needed."

Nathaniel grinned as he snatched a handkerchief from the nightstand and wiped her clean. "What you needed was a good spanking."

"But..."

He silenced her with a kiss. "You're not a child, I know...a fact I can well attest to now." A darkness settled across his features and he pressed his lips into a thin line.

"What's wrong?" Ginny asked as she brushed his hair back, enjoying the way it glided through her fingers.

"You can't stay, Virginia." He pushed away from her to sit on the edge of the bed, his back to her.

She pulled the robe on. Her heart thundered in her chest. She'd known when she'd offered herself to him that he'd not changed his mind, although she held hope he would. "You're going to drop me off at the dock and never look back." Her voice cracked.

"No." He hung his head. "You'll always be there in the back of my mind. I promised I'd take care of you and your brothers." Nathaniel turned to face her, his expression torn between agony and resolve.

Ginny nodded. "I see. Is that all this is then? A debt that needs to be repaid?"

"Your father was as loyal as they come. The least I can do is take care of those whom he loved most."

"What about me? The ones I love." Ginny sat next to him.

"You'll be with your brothers soon." He raked his hand through his hair and stood.

"I wasn't talking about them." She grabbed his wrist and squeezed. When he didn't look at her, she stood and positioned herself in front of him. "Look at me, Nathaniel."

Their gazes met.

Ginny felt the pulse beneath her fingers, their beats synchronizing in the moment. She took a deep breath and licked her lips.

"I want to stay with you because I love you." She wrapped her arms around him when he stood. "You horse's ass. I love you."

His chin settled on the top of her head as he embraced her. A long moment of silence passed between them. When he finally spoke, his words surprised her.

"Virginia, I can't...I can't cage you. If you stayed with me, you wouldn't be free."

"Being the only sister in a brood of boys with no mother and no father. Do you really think I'd be free back in Alton?" She pulled back to glare at him. "They'd probably ship me back east to my grandmother's. She'd marry me off to some nance and I'd be miserable for the rest of my life."

Nathaniel's eyes darkened and his brow furrowed.

"See, you don't like that alternative. But it's the truth. My brothers want me settled as does my aunt and my grandmother." She sighed. "I'm sure they'd frown on your occupation, but you're not a wicked man, Nathaniel. I'm convinced of that, and they will be too."

"What if I can't protect you? I couldn't bear to see you suffer."

Ginny raised her fingers to his lips. "Life's full of danger. But I want to choose my own fate. I want to stay with you." She stood on her tiptoes and kissed the underside of his jaw. "Is me loving you not enough of a reason to let me stay?"

He caught her around the waist and held her eye level before turning to dump her on the bed. When he kissed her, covering her body with his own, she knew the answer before he said it.

"You can stay." He kissed her deeply.

Ginny wrapped her arms around his neck and squealed in delight.

"But there will be rules...limitations." He nipped her neck. "I can't have you running around Baton Rouge without an escort."

"I'm an adult, and believe it or not, I can take care of myself." She jabbed her finger in his chest. "I just need a pistol and a knife."

He pulled back and stared down at her his eyes wide and jaw strung open like a bass. It snapped shut as he shook his head. "You're a hellion. Heaven help anyone who crosses you."

"There are many things you don't know about me,

Nathaniel Blackthorne." She flashed an impish grin.

Nathaniel growled and kissed her again. "I know one thing — you're mine now, Virginia."

CHAPTER ELEVEN

"Sir?" Basset's voice echoed through the door. He knocked again. "Sir, I'm sorry to interrupt..."

Nathaniel groaned as he rolled off of Virginia and reached for his dressing gown. As he pulled it on, he glanced at her. She lay with her hair disheveled, her lips swollen, her body pink and glowing. The girl looked thoroughly debauched and intoxicated by pleasure. *Because of me. Mine.*

"Stay here," he ordered before stealing another kiss. "I'll return in a moment."

"Okay," she murmured, drawing the sheet over herself and curling on her side.

He crossed the room and slipped out the door, being sure to close it firmly behind him. "I hope there's a damned good reason for disturbing me, Basset."

Basset stood at attention, his hands trembling. The man looked close to tears. "Sir, Ms. Pamela is waiting for you in the study. She's — well, you should see for yourself."

Nathaniel had never seen Basset this flustered before. Something had shaken him and whatever it was, it couldn't be good. He dashed past him and headed for his study careless of his current attire.

When he swung the door open, he saw Pamela standing by the window staring out into the street.

"Pamela?" he asked, stepping forward.

Basset closed the door behind him, leaving them alone.

Pamela turned at the sound of his voice. She dropped the handkerchief she held to her mouth revealing a large swollen cut bisecting her lips. As she turned completely, he saw the purple bruise darkening around her right eye. She'd attempted to fix her hair, but the loose chignon hung limply to one side. Strands of ink-like hair draped across her forehead, her eyes smeared with makeup.

He rushed to her side. "What in the devil happened?" He reached out to turn her face to the side, inspecting the damage to her lovely visage.

"Levi...well, we returned to the ship last evening to have a bit of fun." Pamela blushed.

Nathaniel arched his brow but said nothing. It wasn't like her to blush, ever. But knowing the deep affection she'd harbored for Levi for years, it didn't completely shock him.

"When we boarded the ship, they attacked us." Her voice cracked.

"Who attacked you?" Nathaniel took her hand and guided her to the settee by the fireplace. They sat, and he held her hand as she composed herself.

"I'm not sure who they were. They were looking for you, Nathaniel." She met his gaze. "They bound us...then beat us until..." She looked away. "Levi."

"Where is Levi? How did you escape?" Nathaniel tried to be patient with her, but the faster he got answers, the quicker he could deal with the men who'd trespassed on his property and injured his friends.

When Pamela faced him, her eyes were bright with tears. "They still have him." She blinked and the tears stained her cheeks. "He told them I didn't know anything. That I was just a whore—" Her voice broke.

Nathaniel squeezed her hand.

She nodded. "They told me they'd let me go if I—well, you get the point."

"Pamela—"

"One of them took me into the cargo room. While he was trying to unfasten his trousers, I hit him over the head with a crowbar I found lying on one of the cases." She wiped the tears away with her fingers. "I snuck off the ship and walked back to town. I had to tell you." A sob escaped her lips. "I hope he's alive."

Nathaniel drew her into his embrace, stroking her hair. "It's okay. It's over." When she quieted, he pulled back and forced her chin up, meeting her gaze.

"I will find him. I'll take care of this. Those bastards will pay for what they've done."

Pamela nodded and then glanced down at his clothes. She chuckled. "A robe, Nathaniel, at this hour?" A look of realization passed over her face. "Sweet mercy, you bedded her."

"I don't believe that's any of your business." Nathaniel released her and put some space between them.

Her gaze raked down his body then back up. A sudden wave of unease swept over him at her scrutiny.

"I should have known," Pamela said with a chuckle. "Her scent is all over you, sugar."

He cleared his throat and attempted to change the subject. "Let me fetch Nana. She can take care of those cuts and that shiner." He glanced down at her clothes. "Are you hurt anywhere else?"

She waved her hand. "No, I'll be fine. I can take care of this." Her fingers brushed the swollen skin beneath her eye, making her wince.

"I want you to stay here, get cleaned up, and rest. I'll go find Levi." His pointed look warned her against challenging his request.

With hands up in surrender, Pamela stood. "You won't get an argument from me. I haven't slept all night and that walk from the dock damn near killed me."

Nathaniel followed her to the door. He led her upstairs.

"Here's the spare bedroom. If you need anything, please don't hesitate to call Basset." He nodded to the cord hanging by the door. "Poor man was damn near in tears when he told me you were here. You'd better let him help you. He'll cry like a whipped puppy outside your door until you let him."

"I will, miss." Basset poked his head into the room. "Is there anything I can do for you?"

Pamela rolled her eyes. "Of course, Basset. Would you please draw me a bath and then find me something to eat? I'm famished."

"As you wish, miss." Basset disappeared into the adjoining bathroom.

"Told you." Nathaniel grinned. "Have him fetch Nana. She has some salves for that cut. I don't want it to get infected — or scar those gorgeous lips."

"Out with you, scoundrel. You have a woman in your bed who deserves an explanation before you run off."

"I'll find him, Pamela." His voice lowered into a serious tone. "Mark my words."

She nodded and pushed him out of the room. "Go. I'll be fine."

He saw the look of pain cross her face as the door closed. Nathaniel shook his head. How had it all turned upside down? Who dared attack his friends?

When he returned to his bedroom, Virginia lay in the exact same position as she'd assumed before he went downstairs. She was fast asleep. He sighed and decided to leave her in peace. After quickly selecting a few articles of clothing, he retreated into the bathroom.

Washed and dressed less than five minutes later, Nathaniel paused to glance down at her sleeping face. The sheet draped precariously over her breasts, leaving her shoulders exposed. The temptation to kiss her creamy skin and taste her gripped him. He shook his head and balled his hand into a fist. *Later.* He promised himself.

"I love you, kid," he whispered before backing away from the bed.

Nathaniel slipped from the room determined to find the men who dared challenge him. There would be no mercy for their actions against him. None.

Ginny woke with a start. She sighed when the memories of the day's event came flooding back.

"Nathaniel?" she asked rolling over.

An empty bed met her grasping hand. She sat up quickly, her gaze darting around the room.

"Nathaniel?" She snatched her robe and pulled it on before climbing from the bed. Ginny checked the bathroom and the closet, but there was no sign of him.

She pulled the cord by the door to summon Basset. Where could he have gone? Ginny glanced out the window. The sun had already started to set. Perhaps he'd already left to go to the club.

Several moments later, a knock at the door shook her from her thoughts. She opened the door and grinned at the butler. "Have you seen Nathaniel?" she asked, noting Basset's sullen features. "Has something happened?"

"I've got this, Basset," a familiar feminine voice came from behind him.

He stepped to the side revealing Pamela who wore a man's dressing gown, her long hair hanging down.

Ginny blinked twice.

"Pamela, what happened?" The sight of Pamela without makeup made her look...innocent, but that wasn't what drew her attention to Pamela's face. The large cut across her lips and the darkening bruise around her eye made Ginny flinch in sympathetic pain.

Pamela came into the room, shutting the door behind them. She put an arm around Ginny's shoulders and drew her toward the settee at the foot of the bed.

"Sit down, sugar." Pamela pulled her down beside her and sighed.

"Where's Nathaniel?" She swallowed the fear rising in her throat. "Who did this to you?"

Ginny reached out and touched Pamela's swollen cheek.

"A group of men attacked me and Levi on the *Blue Moon*." Pamela took her hand and patted it in an attempt to soothe. "I managed to escape and come here to warn Nathaniel."

"And Levi?" Ginny asked, her hands trembling in both anger and fear.

Pamela shook her head. "I had to leave him behind. Nathaniel will save him." She offered a hesitant smile and winced as it pulled her split lips uncomfortably tight.

"Do you want me to get something for your lip?" Ginny tried to stand but Pamela grabbed her wrist and shook her head.

"I'm fine, sugar. Been beaten worse than this." Her dark eyes clouded for a moment as she stared at the far wall.

"When did he leave?" Ginny glanced out the window. The sun would be fully set in an hour. "Did he say when he would return?"

Pamela turned to face her, shaken from her memory. "I expect he'll return soon. Unless something happened to him."

"We should go to the dock, just to be sure." Ginny stood and rushed over to her trunk, unlocking it and tossing back the lid.

"There's nothing we can do, sugar. Nathaniel left instructions for you to stay here. Basset will never let you leave the house." Pamela paced the room as if conflicted at the thought of whether to go or stay.

"I can't just sit here and wait. What if they were taken? What if they've been injured?"

Ginny refused to speak the fear that haunted the back of her mind. She pulled a pair of trousers from the bottom of the trunk. A special request from when Pamela had ordered her a new wardrobe. She turned to face her mentor. "I love him, Pamela. And I saw the way you looked at Levi. You love him."

"I—" Pamela crossed her arms.

"You can't fool me, sugar." Ginny imitated Pamela's cultured southern tone perfectly. "There's no way we can let them die."

Pamela threw her hands up in surrender. "Fine. But we can't go out there half-cocked and unarmed. Where are we going to get weapons?"

"I don't know. Maybe Thomas or Carl have some at the club. They would have some kind of weapons behind the bar, right?" Ginny paused. "This might sound insane, but I think we can do it."

Ginny crossed to Nathaniel's closet. She pulled out a shirt, trousers, and oversized vest. Laying them on the bed, she glanced at Pamela. "Here. Wear these. Be sure to tuck your hair up and pin it under the cap."

"Do you know what you're doing?" Pamela began to undress.

Ginny pulled the robe off and slipped on the trousers. "I hope so."

Within moments the women were dressed in men's clothes, their hair hidden beneath fishermen's caps. Together they slipped down the staircase.

As they reached the back door, a voice stopped them in their tracks. "I believe you'll need these."

Ginny turned. Basset held out a pair of pistols. She took them, handing one to Pamela.

"Thank you, Basset."

He offered a bag. "Here's the ammunition, should you need more."

She took the bag and slung it over her head so the long strap lay across her chest and the weight of it rested against her hip.

"I have one request, miss." Basset's gaze turned steely. "Bring my master home safely. Don't hesitate to do what must be done."

Ginny nodded and turned to Pamela. "Let's go."

The two women stepped out into the alley. The sun had

dipped below the horizon, leaving the sky streaked with fire and ink.

"How are we going to get to the dock?" Pamela asked.

"We can borrow a car, park away from the dock so they don't hear us coming, then cover the rest on foot." Ginny glanced down the alley.

"Wait here." Pamela ran to the house next door, to the club.

Ginny paced as she waited. "What is that woman doing?"

After a few tense moments, Pamela reappeared. She dangled keys from her fingertips.

"Where did you get those?" Ginny asked in awe.

"Thomas wanted a night with Ginger. I wanted to borrow his truck. Simple trade." Pamela grinned as they walked down to the corner where they found a lovely Ford pick-up.

"You traded sex for his truck?" Ginny shook her head.

"I had something he wanted. He had something I wanted. Life's not as complicated as you'd think, sugar." Pamela slid behind the steering wheel and started the truck.

Ginny climbed in. "I can't argue that logic."

Pamela knew how to get to the dock. For that, Ginny was grateful. She also took comfort in the knowledge that she had someone to back her up. If something went wrong, one of them could go for help. She tried not to think about their fate should they both be captured...or killed.

They parked on a deserted dirt turn-off from the main road headed toward the river about a mile from the dock. The moonlight streamed through the trees, lighting their way.

Ginny glimpsed the three ships sitting at their respective docks. The duo hunched behind the tall, mossy trees in an attempt to catch a glimpse of anyone. A lone, shadowed building stood between them and the river where the *Mississippi Queen* bobbed in the water. The *Sentinel* and the *Blue Moon* stood dark, but flickers of light betrayed life on the

Queen.

"They're still on the *Queen*," Pamela whispered in her ear, drawing the pistol. She took a handful of bullets from the bag and tucked them into her pocket. "We'll get a bit closer and see if we can slip onto the ship."

"Is the gangplank the only way to get on board?" Ginny asked as she strained to see anything. Even with the moonlight aiding her, she couldn't see anything but shadows.

"That's how I escaped. I was lucky I didn't meet anyone when I ran off."

Ginny pondered the situation and then nodded. "We're going to have to split up. I'll go onto the ship while you wait on shore. I'll send you a signal if I need your help. Then you should be able to go for help."

"Don't you mean come help you?" Pamela glanced at her.

With a shrug, Ginny pulled out her gun and made sure it was fully loaded. "If I fire a shot, run for help. If you hear me scream, come save me."

"Why—"

"If there's gunfire, you don't want to go rushing into it. Plus, it's likely one of us has been shot, so it'd be better for you to go get backup." Ginny closed the chamber and spun the cylinder. "If I scream, then that'll be my signal for you to get your ass on the ship."

"Clever." Pamela nodded in agreement. "All right then. I'll wait here. Any closer and I'll be exposed should someone pull up the road or come down off the ship."

The two of them watched the ship for a few minutes, when no one came or went, Ginny grew apprehensive.

"Do you think they're still on the ship?" she whispered.

"Only one way to find out." Pamela tipped the gun up.

"Wait here." Ginny stood and slipped out of the trees.

"Careful, sugar."

Pamela's whispered warning ghosted behind her like the lonesome call of a whippoorwill. Squaring her shoulders,

Ginny tiptoed to the building. She peeked in the dirty windows, finding nothing but darkness. Careful to not make noise, she crept along the building until she faced the ships.

The *Mississippi Queen* stood tall against the midnight sky with the nearly full moon shining down. The familiar, gentle rhythm of the water splashing against the ship and the creak of the hull timbers created a haunting melody.

Ginny glanced up at the windows. Two of them had light, the rest of the ship lay dark. The eerie silence made her wonder if Nathaniel hadn't already taken care of the men and freed Levi. Perhaps their rescue was preemptive. Still, she needed to be sure.

Ginny stole up the gangplank and onto the deck. She leaned against the cabin and took a breath. With a peek to the left, she slid along the wall until she reached the first lit window. Careful to not draw attention to herself, she peered inside.

Two men sat playing cards in the captain's quarters. One had his back to her, but she caught sight of the other man's profile. It was one of the men with the red car! The ones who murdered her father.

A sudden wave of fury threatened to consume her composure. She leaned her head back against the wall and closed her eyes, taking deep breaths until the rage faded into a pulsing ache deep in her chest. She ducked beneath the window and made her way to the next lit room.

The dimmer light shone through the closed shutters. She approached and tried to glance into the room. Nothing. The shutters effectively blocked the contents of the room.

"What do I do now?" she muttered under her breath. "I have to find them."

She backtracked and glanced into every room as she passed. *Empty. Empty. Empty.* She moved to the other side of the ship and took inventory of the rest of the rooms with a quick glimpse. Save for the two men in the captain's quarters, she found no one else aboard the ship.

Not true. You don't know who's in that second room. She had to be sure of who occupied that room. One way to be certain, but first, she had to be sure the men remained in Levi's quarters.

Levi had once told her he had a spare key to his quarters in the wheelhouse, if she ever decided to come stay with him. She shook her head at the silly memory. Levi would have stolen her heart had Nathaniel not done so already. Pamela would have killed her.

She unlatched the door to the wheelhouse and searched the wall near his chair. There, on a little hook, hung the key. After tucking it into her palm, Ginny made her way to his cabin.

With a touch lighter than a pickpocket, she slid the key into the lock and turned it, making sure the bolt slid silently home. She removed the key and tucked it into her pocket. Ginny exhaled, sure her heart would have stopped had they come out and found her there in the hallway. She quickly moved down the hall to the second room, just one door up from the cabin she and Nathaniel had shared less than a week ago.

With one hand, she drew the revolver while she rested the other on the door handle. Quickly, she opened the door and held the revolver aloft, her finger on the trigger. Her gaze swept the room and finally landed on the man lying unconscious on his side on the floor. His dark hair lay across his face, his hands bound with rope. She glanced at his ankles where his feet were tied with the same rope.

"Nathaniel?" she breathed his name as she dropped to her knees and pulled him toward her.

Ginny set the gun beside her and reached for the knife she'd found in the bag with the ammunition. Making quick work of the rope, she massaged his cold wrists and hands.

"We have to get out of here," she whispered. "Wake up, Nathaniel." Ginny gently shook him.

His eyes fluttered open. She sighed in relief when his

gaze landed on her face.

"Virginia," he murmured and then groaned as he attempted to sit up. "What are you doing here?"

"You never came back." She turned his face to the side to inspect the cut near the corner of his lip and the bruise highlighting his strong jaw. "I got worried."

"Are you here alone?" He growled. "You shouldn't be here. If they come back and find you here—"

"They won't, if you hurry," Ginny snapped. Fine thanks he offered when she'd saved his hide. She bit her tongue knowing that an argument at such a moment would only lead to certain capture. "Come on."

Ginny stood and offered him an arm. Once he was on his feet, she scooped up the revolver and gripped it tight as she moved toward the door.

"Where did you get that?" Nathaniel asked, obvious displeasure in his voice.

She chose to ignore it.

"We should go." Ginny glanced at him.

"Wait." He pulled her back into the room. "Tell me you didn't come here alone. And where in the hell did you get that gun?" Nathaniel gripped her arms tight and gave her a shake.

"Pamela came with me. She's in the woods near shore. I told her to wait there for my signal." Ginny cocked her head. "Can we go now?"

"The gun?"

"Ask Pamela."

"Why can't you just tell me where in the hell you got that gun?"

"Does it matter?" Ginny glared at him.

Nathaniel nodded.

"That's my pistol, one of a pair Levi gave me for my birthday." His eyes glinted with concern. "Wait, Levi. Where is he?"

"I couldn't find him," Ginny replied, gripping the pistol tight.

"Did you check the rest of the ship?"

"Yes."

"And there was no sign of Levi?"

Ginny shook her head. "No, I had hoped he was in the room with you. There are two men in the captain's cabin though."

"You came for me when they're just down the hall?" Nathaniel's voice darkened. "You could've been captured."

She pulled the key from her pocket. "I locked them in first."

"Still—" He pushed past her and led the way down the hall until they stepped out onto the deck of the ship near the paddlewheel. They stood in the same alcove where he'd taken her during their excursions on deck what seemed like ages before.

When he was certain they weren't going to be followed, he pulled her into his embrace. "I wouldn't be able to live with myself if anything happened to you."

Nathaniel kissed her and she melted against him. When they broke apart, he sighed. "We have to find Levi."

"Where did they take him?"

He shook his head. "I don't know. They knocked me out when I tried to board the ship. When I came to, I was tied up in that room and they were dragging Levi out of the room."

"Was he dead?" Ginny asked, her heart pounding.

Nathaniel shook his head. "I don't think so. But they refused to keep us in the same room. I heard one of the men saying something about their boss wanting to speak to us separately. I struggled, trying to free myself, and they must have knocked me out again." He rubbed his bruised jaw.

"I recognized one of the men in the captain's quarters," Ginny confessed, her voice barely a whisper. "He was at my farm when..." She fell silent, hoping he would be able to piece the rest together.

"So they're behind this." Nathaniel grit his teeth. "I should have known."

"You know them?" Ginny asked in surprise.

"They're part of a rival gang. Came to me the day you stowed on the ship, asking about a partnership." Nathaniel raked his hand through his hair. "How the hell they found us here—" He shook his head as his voice trailed off.

"What do we do now?" Ginny forced him to focus on the issue at hand.

"Find Levi and then get the bastards who did this." Nathaniel took the gun from her hand.

"Hey." Ginny pouted as he took her weapon. "That's not fair. I'm a decent shot."

"Virginia, a man is not a rabbit or a deer. Have you ever pointed a gun at a man before with the intent to pull that trigger?" Nathaniel stroked his fingers along her face and tipped her chin up to search her eyes. "Have you?"

"Besides you?" she teased.

"You wouldn't have shot me then even if I hadn't stopped my hands from wandering." He chuckled. "You're too fond of me."

"And you're a pompous jackass." She crossed her arms. "I should have let you rot in that room."

Nathaniel brushed his lips against hers. The heat and undeniable pull of him lured her close and she clutched at his jacket.

"Don't go back in there," she whispered against his mouth. "Let's go to town. We'll bring more men back and storm the ship."

"They'll be gone by the time they realize I've escaped." Nathaniel stroked her cheek again. "Get off the ship. I'll take care of them. You and Pamela wait in the woods for me."

"But—" Ginny stopped when the sound of an approaching car echoed against the riverboat.

"They've come." Nathaniel inhaled sharply as the car pulled up to the side of the building, the moonlight reflecting off the hood of the red car.

"Wait here," Nathaniel said, pushing her back against

the wall. "If anything happens to me, I want you to run." He kissed her again, and she clung to him. "Run like hell."

CHAPTER TWELVE

Nathaniel reentered the hallway, carefully making his way toward the room where they'd kept him. He pulled the door closed and proceeded to creep toward the captain's quarters. He heard the footsteps of the men coming up the gangplank. When their boots echoed on the deck, he ducked into the room across from the captain's.

Keeping the door open a crack, he peered out, watching and waiting. He took a breath to steady himself. The gun provided a dose of courage, but the mere knowledge that Virginia was on the ship drove him into a frenzy. He wished her a thousand miles from there — anything to keep her safe.

"Where is he?" A man's voice shattered the silence in the hallway.

Nathaniel tightened the grip on his revolver, his finger a breath from the trigger. Three men approached, one carrying a dark green cloth satchel.

The leader shook the handle of the captain's door. "What the hell?" He pounded on the sturdy wood. "Open this goddamn door."

The men on the inside scuffled and swore as the door shook.

"It's locked from the outside," one of the men inside shouted.

The leader pulled his revolver from his coat and stepped back. "Luke, can you pick the lock?"

The man carrying the satchel stepped forward and reached into his pocket. "Yeah."

He dropped to one knee and pulled a pick from his small kit.

"Where's Blackthorne?" the leader asked through the door.

"He's in the third room down, on the right," came the muffled reply.

Nathaniel took a breath, willing himself to wait for the right moment. He could take them out now, but something stopped him. Hesitation had never been his style, not when it came to protecting his investment, or those he cared about. It was as if a small voice whispered deep inside. *Wait.*

"Go check on Blackthorne." The leader waved his pistol in the direction of the room indicated.

The remaining man darted past them. Nathaniel braced himself for the inevitable. They'd find him missing and all hell would break loose.

The captain's door clicked as the lock slid free. When the door opened, Nathaniel backed away from the crack in the door when the light from the room fell on him.

"He's gone!"

"Where the hell is he?" the leader shouted.

A scuffle ensued and Nathaniel carefully approached the door. The five men had drifted into the captain's quarters. He caught a glimpse of the Garrett brothers and three other men.

"He was here an hour ago. Out cold and strung up tight. There's no way he escaped." Nick Garrett turned to his older brother, Ned.

"Someone helped him escape," Ned growled. "Luke, Sam, go search the ship. If he's still here, find him."

The two men fled the room. Nathaniel made sure to keep himself hidden for fear they'd catch glimpse of him as they passed.

"Where's Blackthorne?" Ned asked again.

"I swear we were here the whole time," Nick replied.

"Even him?" Ned gestured with the revolver.

Nathaniel heard the slamming of doors as they checked

every room down the hall.

"Yeah, he's been here the whole time." Nick crossed his arms.

"I don't trust him."

"I don't trust you," a third, more familiar voice added.

Nathaniel stopped breathing. His hand trembled and his heart seized. *It can't be.* Then he heard her scream. Time stopped as the pieces of the puzzle fell into place.

"Let me go, you rotten, murdering bastards!" Virginia struggled as the two men dragged her down the hall and tossed her into the room.

"Well, well, look what we have here, boys. The dame has come to rescue her keeper." Ned grabbed her by the arm. "Where is he?"

Ginny stumbled into the room, colliding with one of the men. He reached out to steady her. When she met his gaze, she gasped.

"Levi?" she whispered. A shard of ice cold dread pierced her gut.

"Well, well, look what we have here, boys. The dame has come to rescue her keeper." One of the men grabbed her by the arm, pulling her away from Levi. "Where is he?"

Ginny winced at the pain of his grip but refused to budge. "Go to hell." She spat on him.

"Blackthorne obviously hasn't shown you any discipline." He jerked her closer. "Guess I'll have to remedy that."

"Let her go, Ned. She wasn't part of this deal," Levi interjected.

"Well, since the man I wanted to see is now missing, I'll keep her as a consolation prize." Ned grinned as he released her arm. "Sit down," he instructed her.

Ginny reluctantly flopped down onto a chair near the wall and crossed her arms.

"Are you hurt?" Levi asked, reaching for her.

"Traitor. I hope you burn in hell for betraying him." Ginny backed away from his touch and fumed at the man she'd thought was a friend and ally.

Levi sighed and turned back to the other men. "You promised no one else would be involved."

"I would have kept that promise. Unless you bring me Blackthorne, she's mine."

Ginny bit her tongue to keep from reacting to his threat. She felt the bag slip against her hip. *The knife.* She sat up straight and shifted to slide her hand into the bag without notice. Her hand closed around the comforting handle of the blade.

Levi shook his head and scratched his chin beneath his beard. "He wouldn't have left her willingly. He has to be on the ship."

"I am." Nathaniel stepped into the doorway, his revolver raised. "Don't even think about reaching for those guns." He motioned to the left side of the room with the barrel. "Over there, all of you. Slowly, with your hands in the air."

"Nathaniel—" Levi began but stopped speaking when Nathaniel glared at him.

"I'll deal with you later." He cocked the pistol. "Virginia, come here."

Their eyes met as she rose from her seat and moved past one of the men, trying to ignore the flutter of fear churning in her stomach. Before she could react, Ginny was firmly pressed against Ned with a cold gun barrel digging into her temple.

"You have something I want, Blackthorne, and it's not this tempting little morsel here."

"Let her go. I swear by all that's holy, if you harm a hair on her head, I will gut you and your men myself and not a soul alive will find your corpses." His voice had deepened, the timbre reverberating deep into her bones.

Dangerous, dark…this was the side of him she'd never seen. It terrified her, and yet, knowing it was her safety that triggered this beast inside of him thrilled her.

His hand encircled her throat. "You're all talk, Blackthorne. Everyone knows this. You've been running booze for what, ten years now, and not once have you ever followed through on your threats."

"No one has ever dared to call my bluff." The gun never wavered in Nathaniel's hand.

Ginny's grip tightened on the knife. She could try to give Nathaniel the opportunity he needed to shoot. The gun barrel dug into her scalp just above her ear.

"I'm calling it now." Ned paused for a heartbeat. "Your days as a shine runner are over. I'm taking control of your route."

"Over my dead body." Nathaniel chuckled. The hollow and haunting sound caused Ginny to shiver.

"I figured that was the stipulation." Ned's hand caressed her throat, sliding down into her shirt. "Don't worry, I'll take good care of her when you're gone."

Virginia grimaced at the action, her gaze locked with Nathaniel's. He ground his teeth, the muscle in his jaw clenching as his finger twitched on the trigger. Ginny took the opportunity to draw the blade from the bag, careful to keep it by her side so the men wouldn't see it. Nathaniel's gaze drifted down and then back to her eyes.

"Not if I take care of you first," Nathaniel replied as he nodded to Ginny.

Ned's hand squeezed her breast as the barrel pressed to her temple. "Don't call me out. I will kill her."

A deep rumble shook the boat. She rocked beneath their feet as she woke from her rest, causing them all to sway. His hand slipped from her shirt and grabbed her waist before she could break free.

"What was that?" Ned asked, his voice sharp.

"The boiler," Levi said as his eyes widened. "But who?"

"Search the ship again! There's someone else aboard," Ned snapped at his brother and the spare goons. "Find them!"

They darted from the cabin, leaving Levi and Ned to face Nathaniel. Ginny wiggled in an attempt to wrench herself from Ned's grasp. Her grip tightened on the knife when he pulled her against him.

"Enough games, Blackthorne, put the gun down or I kill your little bitch."

The sound of gunfire echoed somewhere on the ship. Nathaniel's eyes locked with Ginny's. When he nodded, she drove the blade into Ned's side.

He howled in pain.

Ginny stole the distracted moment and shoved herself away from him, tripping and dropping to the floor. She turned in time to see Nathaniel pull the trigger before Ned could even raise his weapon. The gunshot stung her ears, muffling the sound of the boat.

Ned dropped the gun before collapsing to the floor in a stunned, bloody heap.

Nathaniel turned the pistol on Levi.

"I'm sorry." The gun shook in Levi's hand.

Time seemed to stand still as they stood, revolvers aimed at the other's hearts.

Ginny climbed to her feet and came up behind Nathaniel. Levi could have shot her. He could have easily shot Nathaniel before, but he didn't. It seemed there might be more to the story than met the eye.

"Nathaniel." She rested her hand on his shoulder.

"What in the blue blazes is going on in here?" Pamela's shrill exclamation broke the silence but seemed to enhance the tension.

"Levi has some explaining to do." Nathaniel lowered his gun. "Where are the other two?"

"Out cold. Tied them up in the boiler room." Pamela turned to Levi. "You'd best lower that weapon if you know what's good for you."

Levi dropped the gun and set it on the table. He refused to meet either Pamela or Nathaniel's gazes. But when he caught Ginny's, a sad smile crept across his lips. *Sorry, love,* he mouthed before clearing his throat and turning to Pamela.

"I heard everything," she said. The chill in her voice could have frozen the Gulf of Mexico.

"I figured you did." Nathaniel tucked his gun away.

"What are you going to do with him?" Pamela asked as she approached Levi. Ginny noticed the derringer in her hand for the first time.

"I don't know." Nathaniel ran his hand through his hair before turning to Ginny and opening his arms.

Ginny buried herself against him, inhaling his scent, thankful that they both had survived somehow.

"Let me take care of it."

Pamela's words sent a chill through Ginny. Fear flashed in Levi's eyes. Double crossing Nathaniel was one thing, but it seemed that crossing Pamela could prove even more dangerous.

"One stipulation, Pamela," Nathaniel said clearly. "You can't kill him."

Pamela inclined her head in reluctant agreement. "Let Lydia know she's in charge until I return. Oh, and I'm borrowing your boat. I'll be sure to clean up." A humorless half-smile hung on her lips as she pressed the gun barrel to Levi's ribs. "Come on, sugar. We have unfinished business."

Nathaniel nodded to Pamela and glared at Levi before shaking his head. He took Ginny by the hand and pulled her from the room. Halfway down the corridor, Ginny shook her hand free.

"We're just going to leave them here?" she asked, dumbstruck. "Aren't you the least bit curious as to why he betrayed you?"

"I have a feeling I know the reason behind it, but Pamela will be sure to let me know as soon as she's finished with him." Nathaniel grabbed her hand and pulled her out into the night air, down the gangplank, and closer to the red Ford Roadster.

The sound of the paddlewheel splashing in the water made her glance over her shoulder. The *Mississippi Queen* pulled away from the shore and gently began her ascent up the mighty river. A soft glint of moonlight played off the wake rippling through the water.

"Where are they going?" Ginny asked as she turned to Nathaniel.

Instead of a reply, Nathaniel wrapped his arms around Ginny and pulled her into a warm, loving embrace. His lips brushed the top of her head, and she tipped her chin up.

"But I want to know why in the hell Levi turned on you." Her body hummed from the danger and excitement.

"I'll tell you later. Let's get home first."

Being in Nathaniel's arms made her acutely aware of the fact that she could have lost him forever. A tear slipped over her cheek. She brushed it away and sniffed. *I won't cry,* she chastised herself.

"Come on, let's get you home, kid," he said as he brushed his thumb across her lower lip.

"But—" She tried to glance back at the river, but he cupped her cheek and turned her attention on him.

Nathaniel silenced her with a soft kiss. She melted against him.

"Trust me," he whispered.

Ginny nodded and climbed into the Roadster at his prompting. The engine roared to life. She sighed as they wove down the dirt road. The weight of the evening crushed down on her.

"Close your eyes and rest."

"I couldn't possibly sleep after that," Ginny said with a yawn. Her eyes grew heavy as the Roadster lulled her and exhaustion finally claimed her.

Someone was carrying her. She opened her eyes and saw

the sharp line of Nathaniel's jaw. Reaching up, she brushed her fingers along the stubble highlighting his face.

He glanced down at her. "I didn't mean to wake you."

"I didn't realize I'd fallen asleep." Ginny snuggled against the warmth of his chest. "Are we home?"

"No." Nathaniel laid her on a soft surface.

Ginny sat up, taking in the unfamiliar surroundings. A small room with rustic furniture and a comfortable lived in feeling. She fisted her hand in the patchwork quilt on the bed beneath her.

"Where are we?" she asked finally meeting his gaze.

"A safe house on the River Road heading north to Memphis."

Surprised, Ginny jumped up and glanced out the window. The sun was setting.

"I slept all day?"

When she turned, Nathaniel had collapsed on the bed fully clothed.

"Yes," he mumbled beneath his arm as it lay draped across his face.

"What about the club? And Pamela?" Ginny fiddled with the hem of her vest.

"Virginia, sit down." Nathaniel sat up and pulled her onto his lap. "I've taken care of the club and left instructions for Thomas to deliver to Pamela's girls." He tipped her chin toward him and kissed her lips softly.

The tension melted out of her at his tender touch. Ginny sighed as he broke the kiss and leaned his forehead to hers. He pulled back and motioned to a basket on the table. "Nana packed us some food for the trip if you're hungry."

Ginny glanced at the basket then back at him. "Where are we going?" Ginny feared she already knew the answer.

"I'm taking you home to your brothers." He sighed. "Seeing him press that gun to your head, knowing that one false move would be your end." Nathaniel held her close, his grip possessive and desperate. "I can't put you in a position like that again."

"So you're just going to dump me at some house in Alton and walk away, leaving me there to rot away like an old spinster." She pushed him away and tried to scoot off his lap.

His grip tightened around her. "Then how do I make this work? How can I be sure you'll be safe with me?"

"You can't. No one can tell the future, Nathaniel." Ginny softened against him again and toyed with his shirt collar. "I can't promise I won't stay out of trouble if you leave me to my own devices."

"I could make your brothers take turns watching you."

"Pa tried that. Never worked. My brothers know better than to try to keep me locked away." Ginny grinned up at him. "I'll do what I want anyway."

"You're a hellion, Virginia. Has anyone ever told you that?"

"You have...several times." She winked at him. "The only way you can guarantee my safety is if you keep me by your side. Simple."

"The way you say it makes me think life may never be *simple* with you in tow." He kissed her again.

Ginny twisted in his lap so her arms wrapped around his neck, drawing him closer, deepening the kiss. She tasted the bitter tang of coffee and the sweet seductive flavor uniquely his own. Nathaniel groaned and pulled her down on top of him as he lay back on the bed. Their kiss became frenzied as they grasped at each other's clothing. He slipped the vest off her shoulders, then unbuttoned the shirt, slipping the hem from her pants. When he opened the shirt, she whimpered at the cool air brushing against her bare breasts.

He took a nipple in his mouth, suckling and teasing. Ginny fisted her hands in his hair. His scruff brushed the sensitive skin. She wanted more.

Pulling back for a moment, Ginny stripped the rest of her clothes off and settled herself astride his thighs. He settled back against the blankets and watched her, hunger consuming his expression. His eyes flashed dark with need as she reached for his belt.

Playful, she loosened the belt and unfastened his pants. He groaned as she slipped them down, freeing his cock. She took him in her hands and stroked him. His hands covered hers.

"Inside you," he murmured, drawing her up to kiss her lips again.

He guided her as she lowered herself onto him. A calm settled around them as the moment lingered. Neither of them moved.

"I love you, Nathaniel," she whispered.

He rocked his hips, driving up into her. A cry escaped from deep within her as the pleasure surged forward. She took his lead and moved, grinding her hips, letting a sensual rhythm take control. His fingers dug into her hips, urging her forward.

Mindless, she rode him. Her body reveled in the control, in the sensations leading her toward completion. His hands wandered across her skin. She writhed against him, her body aflame.

When he thrust into her again, Ginny unraveled at the pleasure that burst through her. She collapsed on top of him, her breathing ragged and hoarse. As she slowly recovered, Nathaniel rolled her onto her back and slid inside her again.

"I'm not finished with you yet, darlin'." He kissed her as he made love to her slowly.

Her climax had only heightened her senses. Every stroke brought her body sparking to life. She moaned his name and licked her lips. Her body moved on its own, arching into his thrusts, pulling him closer, deeper. When blissful release washed over her again, Nathaniel followed with his own, filling her completely.

Limbs entangled, sweat slickened, and blissfully exhausted, Nathaniel and Ginny lay together in the quiet room. His hand absently traced a path along her arm as he lay half atop her.

"No more arguments now." Ginny broke the silence.

"About?" he grumbled, half asleep.

"Leaving me behind."

He pulled her closer, if that were possible. "I couldn't if I tried."

"Damned right." She grinned and snuggled against him.

Ginny sighed when she heard the soft strains of snoring beside her. She pressed a kiss to his cheek. "You're lucky I love you."

CHAPTER THIRTEEN

The rest of the drive proved uneventful. When Nathaniel pulled up to the fashionable part of town, Ginny practically leaned out the window admiring the lovely tree-lined streets and quiet neighborhood. She turned to him, her expression radiant.

"Are we almost there?" she asked, voice bubbling with excitement.

"Yes," he said as he shook his head in wonder. How could this plucky young woman be such a damned temptress and an innocent all wrapped into one? Even after the last few weeks, it felt as though he'd seen every possible side of her. Yet, here was something new.

They pulled up in front of a multicolored Victorian home situated on a quiet corner. The white picket fence lining the sidewalks ran alongside the dark shrubbery landscaping the yard. A pair of sycamores stood sentinel in the corner of the lot giving the house ample shade.

Ginny practically leapt from the car as soon as he put it in park and turned off the engine. She bounced on her toes as he rounded the back of the car.

"Gin!" a masculine voice called from the porch of the house.

"Eric!" Ginny ran to the gate and wrenched it open.

"She's here!" he shouted into the house through the screen door before running down the steps. Eric swept his sister up into his arms, hugging her tight.

"I'm so glad you're okay," Ginny said before burying her

face in his neck.

Nathaniel latched the gate behind him, lingering back to give the brothers their reunion with their sister. A fierce protectiveness surged through him as he saw the tears streaming down her face. Her smile quelled the need for him to reach for her.

A stampede burst through the front door of the house. Five young men suddenly circled around Virginia, effectively cutting him out of the moment.

Nathaniel counted them again. *Six.* He smiled. It seemed as though C.R. Evans had followed through with his promise to locate the other brothers after all.

As he watched the reunion, the overlap of voices and excitement became too much for him. Nathaniel donned his hat and stepped back through the gate. He climbed into the red Ford and started the engine.

Before he could put it in drive, Virginia appeared outside his window pounding furiously on the glass. He rolled it down before she put her fist through it.

"Where are you going?" she asked, breathless.

"I'll leave you to catch up with your brothers. I have to go talk to my solicitor." He smiled at her. "Don't worry, love. I'll be back for dinner."

Virginia grinned at him. "I'll fry you up some fish."

Nathaniel wrinkled his nose. "How about steak?" He pulled out his wallet and handed her some money. "This should cover everyone."

"Thank you," Virginia said as she leaned through the window and kissed him.

A chorus of cat calls and whistles echoed through the open passenger window.

"Shut your traps!" Virginia shouted over the roof of the car. She leaned down to Nathaniel again. "See you in a little while then, sugar."

She sauntered away, her hips swaying as she blew him a kiss over her shoulder.

Nathaniel shook his head. Pamela certainly made an impression on her it seemed. He waved to the sentry of brothers standing around her and pulled away from the curb. They disappeared into the house as he drove away.

Taking his time, Nathaniel wove through the streets until he reached the offices of C.R. Evans, Attorney-at-Law. He parked on a side street, as not to draw attention with the flashy car.

When he knocked on the door, Nathaniel couldn't shake the sense of uncertainty that had taken root in his chest. *Am I doing the right thing?*

The door opened revealing Evans. The dapper lawyer flashed his pearly whites and offered his hand in greeting. "Blackthorne! I didn't know you were in town. Come in."

Nathaniel shook his hand and entered the office suite. "Just got into town."

"Have a seat." Evans gestured to one of the wing-backed leather chairs. "Want some coffee?"

"Black, please." Nathaniel admired his slick-haired blond friend.

Evans had been one of his first investors when he'd begun his venture. They'd been through hell over the last ten years, but the profits eased any temporary setbacks. Levi was the only friend he'd had longer. The sting of that betrayal still burned.

Nathaniel took the cup Evans offered. "Thank you."

"How's business?" Evans asked, sitting down in the chair opposite Nathaniel.

"Business is hot. Although we may have run into another set of complications." He took a sip of coffee and set the cup down on the end table.

"Is the girl okay?" Evans leaned forward, his brow creased with concern.

"She's fine for now. I dropped her off with her brothers. Thank you for that, by the way. It seems as though you went above and beyond to find the two who went missing."

Evans shook his head. "I found them totally by chance. I'd gone down to the precinct to take care of a client who'd gotten himself into trouble with the prohi officers. One of the young recruits came in toting these two belligerent boys yammering on about the Garrett brothers and how they needed to find their sister." He leaned back in his chair. "I placed a few inquiries and had them released into my care. Lucky break, huh?"

"What had happened to them?"

"After the Garrett brothers killed their pa, they took those two boys and beat them for nearly two weeks trying to get information about their father's shine stills and your involvement." Evans frowned, but it dissipated as he continued. "Once I told them their sister was safe and returned them to their brothers, they gave me everything I need to file an official inquiry into those two rat bastards."

Nathaniel stared at him in disbelief. He shook himself, preparing to tell Evans the bad news on that count. "I'm just glad they're all together again."

"How's Levi?" Evans asked.

"He's a traitor." Nathaniel cut to the heart of the problem. "He'd sold me out to the Garrett brothers. If it wasn't for Pamela and Virginia, I'd be feeding the fish at the bottom of the river."

Evans' eyes widened in shock.

"I can't believe it. Levi's always been loyal." He slumped in his chair, stroking his chin in thought. "What would have made him tip over the edge like that? Especially to a couple of rats like the Garretts."

"I need you to do some digging for me and find out." Nathaniel shook his head. "I have a feeling it might have been some old debts that came into play. Levi always had a soft spot for cards, but Lady Luck never favored him."

"I'll see what I can find." Evans pulled out a notepad and scribbled on it. "Where is he now?"

"On the *Mississippi Queen*, sailing upriver from Baton

Rouge."

"You still let him do his run, even after that?" Evans stared at Nathaniel, his jaw gaping.

Nathaniel shook his head. "Pamela's got him tied up at the moment."

"She's interrogating him, you mean?"

"You know their history. When she found out he'd sold us upriver—well, she wouldn't take no for an answer." Nathaniel shrugged.

"You sure she won't kill him?"

"I honestly don't know. Those two have been stupid in love with each other for years. She might torture the hell out of him, but I doubt she'll pull the trigger."

Evans cleared his throat. "Anything else I should know about?"

"Yeah, you might want to call off the inquiry into the Garrett brothers. They're dead. I drove their car all the way up here from Baton Rouge."

"Son of a bitch, Nathaniel. How am I supposed to protect your assets if you don't take this seriously?" He ran his hand through his slick hair, mussing it completely.

"I do take this seriously." Nathaniel leaned forward in his chair. "They attacked the Chapman farm, kidnapped two of the boys and beat information out of them, then drove to my dock over a thousand miles downriver and took control of my ship threatening the woman I love! I did what I had to do and I don't regret a single, solitary action."

"That's total bullshit and you know it—wait, did you say *the woman you love*?" Evans dropped the pen on the notepad.

"Yeah, I did." The realization slammed into Nathaniel like a steam locomotive. He scowled at Evans who was looking at him as though he'd just sprouted a third head.

"I never imagined you'd fall for the girl." He stood and walked around the desk. "Well then, hot damn, it looks like there may be a bright ray of sunshine in this shit storm." Evans opened the drawer and pulled out a flask and two glasses.

"What are you doing?" Nathaniel asked as he rose to his feet.

"Celebrating. I never thought I'd see the day where you'd say those words." Evans poured two drinks and handed one to Nathaniel. "To the girl who felled the mighty Blackthorne."

After he downed the shot, Nathaniel set the glass down. "I wouldn't say that."

"What do you mean?" Evans set his empty glass on the desk.

He pulled the keys from his pocket and set them on the fine mahogany. "Here's the keys to the Garretts' Ford. It's parked in the alley. Get rid of it."

"Where are you going?" Evans asked, worry lacing his tone. "You're not leaving her here, are you?"

"I've set aside enough funds to take care of those kids. Keep an eye on them for me, would you?" Nathaniel slid his fedora on, pulling it down tight.

"I can't believe you'd do that to the woman you love." Evans grabbed him by the shoulders and shook him. "What am I supposed to tell them...her?"

"Tell her I'm sorry." Nathaniel shrugged his shoulders and Evans' hands dropped. "Keep her safe for me." He stalked to the door and rested his hand on the knob when Evan's voice stopped him cold.

"Coward. If you really cared about that girl, you'd do right by her. You might be the best shine runner on the Mississippi River, but you're a lout if you abandon the one woman who cracked that stone you call a heart."

"I'll be in touch. You know how to contact me." Nathaniel walked out the door and into the street.

A gnawing ache settled in his chest as he wandered down the street to the warehouse he owned by the dock where his Lincoln awaited...and his uncertain future on the streets of Baton Rouge.

"You going to milk that gigglewater all night, boss?" Thomas asked as he wiped the bar. He cast Nathaniel sidelong glances.

"Don't you have work to do?" Nathaniel snapped and finished the liquid lingering in the bottom of his glass.

Thomas moved closer. "Yeah, don't you?"

Nathaniel glared at him.

"That girl got under your skin, boss. Admit it—missing her is what's got you all in a sour mood."

"If you want to keep your gig, I suggest you shut your yap, kid." Nathaniel pushed the glass toward Thomas.

Without hesitation, Thomas filled it with bourbon he had stashed under the bar.

One of the new girls stepped out onto the stage and began singing a sultry blues number. Nathaniel watched her for a moment, his mind picturing Virginia on that stage, wearing the midnight purple gown, her auburn and gold hair pinned into a sleek coiffeur. He blinked twice and looked down into his glass before taking the shot of liquor.

The club had gotten hotter as the summer wore on. Word of the Nightingale of New Orleans had spread through the state and drawn a crowd. Their disappointment at her absence vanished when he hired several new girls to wait tables and take turns singing on stage. But they weren't Virginia.

He'd left her with her brothers in Alton, where she'd be safe. And damn if that decision didn't sting like hell every day. She must have hated him when he never came home for dinner. Not that he could blame her. It was a lousy thing to do. He deserved every ounce of misery, but she deserved better than a life on the run and an old man like him.

"Boss," Thomas whispered as he nudged Nathaniel in the ribs. "Look." He pointed to the door where Carl stood watch.

Nathaniel glanced up to see Carl's broad back. When the bouncer stepped aside, his heart stopped.

Draped in emerald green velvet, Virginia stepped into the Casa de Luna. Her hair flowed over her shoulders like a soft, silken, copper-tinted waterfall. When she smiled at Carl and handed him her wrap, she damn near glowed. Her gaze drifted, landing with a punch right on Nathaniel.

He sat rooted to his spot in the corner of the bar. *What in the blue blazes is she doing here?* Then he spotted her older brother, Eric, behind her wearing a smart pinstripe suit and black fedora with a white stripe. The kid cleaned up well, he'd give them that. But it didn't explain what the hell they were doing in Baton Rouge standing in his club.

Although, it didn't take a genius to figure out why they'd come.

"Go to her, boss," Thomas murmured.

Before Nathaniel could respond or even move, she crossed the floor, heading for the stage. The crowd parted around her as whispers began to murmur through the crowd. The poor girl singing on stage stopped mid-croon as Virginia took the stage.

She murmured something in the girl's ear. Gracefully, the young woman hugged Virginia and turned to the crowd, her face flushed with a smile on her lips.

"Ladies and gentleman, it is my pleasure to present the Nightingale of New Orleans singing *Have You Ever Been Lonely?*" She stepped aside, clapping along with the crowd, as Virginia stepped up to the microphone.

Nathaniel gaped for a moment before snapping his mouth closed. The girl had some clout. She waltzed into his club, bold as brass, and took the stage as though it belonged to her. He shook his head.

Her sweet voice rang through the silent crowd. She captured everyone's attention. Nathaniel had to smile. She certainly caught his.

"That was a pretty lousy thing you did, Blackthorne," a man murmured next to him.

He hadn't even realized her brother had taken the seat next to him. Nathaniel glanced at him and motioned for Thomas. He tapped his glass and pointed to the kid.

Thomas nodded and poured a drink for Eric. After sliding it in front of him, Thomas left them alone.

"Thanks." Eric picked up the drink and sipped it, his attention fixed on his sister.

Nathaniel nodded before glancing back at the stage. Virginia's voice slid over his skin, heating his blood and bringing sinful thoughts to the front of his mind. Thoughts of bright moonlight and bare flesh, warm water and hot summer night air.

"I know why you did it," Eric said, snapping the erotic thoughts pooling in his head. "But she deserved better, you know. Better than you just dumping her on our doorstep and leaving without so much as a goodbye."

He took a drink as the kid spoke. The guilt twisted in his gut.

"She broke every piece of china in the house when you never came back. The next day she locked herself in her room when we wouldn't let her leave the house to look for you." Eric took a breath. "She climbed out the window and down the side of the house when she realized we were keeping guard. Took us three days to find her after that."

Nathaniel finished the bourbon in one swallow and stared at the woman on stage. The tenacious, wild, feisty woman he'd fallen in love with. He shook his head again.

"When I finally found her, she'd cornered Mr. Evans and threatened him with physical violence if he didn't tell her exactly where you'd gone and why you'd left. It took three of us to drag her off of him." Eric chuckled and took a drink. "She threatened to walk all the way to Baton Rouge, so I offered to drive her. At least then I could be sure she made it safely. Once she makes up her mind, there's no stopping her."

"That's true," Nathaniel added.

The song drifted to an end and a chorus of cheers and applause rocked the club. Virginia took a bow and leaned down to say something to the band. The musicians nodded and struck up another song. The crowd fell silent once more as she stepped up to the mic.

The familiar strains of *It's All Forgotten Now* floated through the air. Nathaniel groaned. She had to be purposely choosing songs that damn near broke his heart.

When their eyes locked across the smoky room, she poured every ounce of emotion into the song. The atmosphere, the people melted into the background, leaving them as though they were the only two souls in the room.

He listened to the words, to her voice as it spoke to the deepest part of his heart. Like a bolt from the blue, he realized the truth.

Her gaze lingered for a moment longer before returning to the crowd who sat entranced by her performance. Without a word, Nathaniel pushed away from the bar and retreated to the safe, quiet of his office. Once the door clicked shut, he leaned against it. Her soft melody drifted through the wood and he closed his eyes.

"You know you're a damned fool." He ran his hand through his hair.

The riot of applause echoed on the other side of the wall. Nathaniel pushed away and sat down in his office chair. If he went back out there in the midst of the crowd, he'd gravitate toward her. She'd be swarmed with admirers. He'd make a damned fool of himself.

Virginia would find him—if her appearance at the club that night was any indication. But he wouldn't underestimate her. Even though her songs spoke of love, a girl like her wouldn't forgive and forget so quickly. Her sultry glances hid a challenge, one he'd have to accept.

He picked up an invoice laying on his desk and tried to focus on the numbers. But the booze and her presence created a riot throughout his body. He couldn't concentrate. Pinching the bridge of his nose, Nathaniel took a deep breath.

A soft knock at the door finally pushed him to put down the paper.

"Come in," he called out.

Virginia swept into the room, her emerald gown shimmering in the low light. When she turned to face him, he eyed the deep *v* of her gown as it emphasized her breasts. He hadn't noticed how perfect the dress clung to her, or how much he wanted to peel the fabric from her body.

She took a few steps closer, leaning against the edge of his desk.

Nathaniel let his eyes wander. When they returned to meet hers, he recognized the heat simmering in their depths.

"Is that all I get from you?" she asked, her voice husky and sweet. "The cold shoulder."

He sat still as she rounded the desk and spun him to face her. She leaned close, resting her hands on the arms of the chair, pinning him there.

At eye level, her breath brushed against his lips. It took every ounce of willpower not to kiss her, but he had to wait, let it play out on her terms. She needed the control. Virginia deserved that much.

When she drew back and slapped him, the sting hurt his pride more than his face.

"How could you leave me like that?" Her voice wavered. He saw the pain and anger churning inside of her. "I thought we had an understanding, damn it."

He bit his tongue as she pushed on.

"After everything we've been through, you still think you know what's best for me. You think leaving me with my overprotective brothers is what I want." Virginia searched his face, her lip trembling as she spoke. "I should walk out that goddamned door and find someone else who's willing to treat me as an adult...as a lover."

"I've been alone for a long time, Virginia." He began,

knowing she deserved the truth. "Since I left England twelve years ago."

Nathaniel stared at her, watching the way her eyes flashed with fury and pain.

"Is that what you wanted?" She crossed her arms. "To be alone."

He nodded. "It made me stronger."

"Is that what you want now?" Her jaw set harsh against the soft lines of her face.

Nathaniel hung his head. "Honestly, I want you safe. I wouldn't be able to live with myself if you came to harm because of me."

She uncrossed her arms and reached for him before quickly retracting her hand. "Does this have anything to do with Sarah?"

Her name on Virginia's lips startled him. "Who—"

"Pamela mentioned her name, but nothing more." Virginia straightened to her full height and locked gazes with him.

Nathaniel reached for her, but she pulled away.

"You don't love me. That much was clear when you walked away leaving me to wonder what the hell had happened to you." Virginia shook her head and backed away. "When I walk out that door, I can promise you'll never see me again." She turned and stormed for the door.

He followed and slammed his hand against the door as she reached for the handle.

"Sarah and I grew up together. Her family's estate was near my parent's. When I returned from the war, we courted. Hell, I even proposed to her."

He stared at Virginia's profile as she turned her head to the side, listening to him. Her curves and warmth held him captive.

"What happened?" Virginia asked softly.

"I caught her with another man a week before the wedding." The memory assaulted him as he recounted the moment his life shattered. "I left England on the day we were supposed to be married."

"You left everything you loved because of her?"

Nathaniel shook his head. "I left because the man I'd found her with was my eldest brother." He scoffed. "She wanted the title more than she wanted me. I never told my parents what had happened. I packed my belongings and bought a ticket for America. I wanted no part in that kind of life. Having to play nicely with my brother and his wife, who both ripped my heart out."

"Do you regret it?" She licked her lips. "Leaving?"

He thought for a moment, trying to ignore the allure of the woman before him and how much he'd missed her.

"I regret not telling my parents why I left." He pushed forward, "But had I not left, I wouldn't have found you."

Virginia sucked in a breath and shivered.

When she spun to face him, he pushed her against the wall, his hands on her waist. Their lips dangerously close to touching.

"You're not walking out that door, Virginia." Nathaniel brushed his nose against hers in a feather light caress. "I was a damned fool for walking away...for not listening to you. For that, I apologize." Her fathomless eyes sparkled at his words. "I love you, and I'll be damned if I spend the rest of my life wondering if you're happier without me."

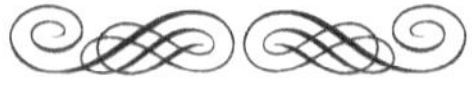

She blinked back the tears at his confession and buried her hands in his hair. "Was that so hard to say?"

Nathaniel punished her with a bruising kiss. She knew if she pushed him hard enough, he'd come to the right conclusion. She moaned when he brushed her tongue with his. Opening for him, she poured herself into the moment. She'd missed him, yearned for him. Being back in his embrace felt like coming home. His arms locked around her, dragging her back until he collapsed on the couch, pulling her on top of him.

"Of all the ships in all the world, you had to stow away on mine," Nathaniel teased as he nipped along her jaw. He grabbed fistfuls of her skirt, dragging the material up, exposing her thighs and the tops of her stockings.

When his warm touch skimmed her inner thighs, she inhaled sharply and shifted to straddle his legs. She grinned when he touched the place where her panties should have been.

His eyes widened as he stroked her lower lips. "No drawers. You are a damn temptress now."

"I blame you," she whispered as she reached between them and unbuckled his pants. Slipping his cock free of the fabric, she settled on his lap so he pushed at her entrance.

She lowered herself, taking him completely. Her fingers grasped his lapels as her lips crashed against his. He thrust up as she rocked her hips against him. Faster until the pressure overwhelmed her, and she tipped into a warm sensual pool of pleasure. His groans became incoherent words against her skin as he found his own release. He pressed a soft kiss to her throat.

Ginny met his languid gaze. "I missed you." She brushed her lips against his, letting it grow into a deep, soulful kiss.

Nathaniel sighed as they broke apart. He pushed her hair back over her shoulder, letting his fingertips trail against her bare skin.

She shivered beneath his touch.

"I missed you too," he murmured. "I'm glad you came back."

"I love you, Nathaniel Blackthorne." She pressed a finger to his chest, just above his heart. "But if you ever pull that bushwa with me again, I'll put a bullet through you."

"Don't worry, sweetheart." He laughed and kissed her pursed lips. "I love you too much to let you end up in prison."

"What happens now?" Ginny asked and started laughing when she realized they were still joined and half in dishabille. "I guess we should clean up and rejoin the patrons in the other room."

"Or we could stay here until everyone goes home and have our own little celebration." Nathaniel winked.

A pounding at the door interrupted their conversation.

"I guess that answers that," Nathaniel grumbled as he pushed Ginny off his lap and fixed his pants. He peeked through the door and spoke quietly.

Ginny tidied herself with a handkerchief and straightened her gown. She moved to the mirror to fix her hair when Nathaniel rejoined her.

He wrapped his arms around her waist. "Your brother has volunteered to sing the next song. I think he may have had one too many drinks on the house."

"Let him sing. He's damn good, but he's never sung in front of anyone before. It'll be good for him."

"Are you certain?" he asked with a concerned expression. "I don't know."

"Trust me." Ginny turned and pressed a kiss to his cheek. "It might be good for business."

Hand in hand, Ginny led Nathaniel back into the club. The upbeat melody began to play.

Eric stood center stage, his eyes closed, as he began to sing. A familiar tune made Ginny smile. It was her favorite song, *Ain't Misbehavin'*.

"I'll be damned, the kid can sing." Nathaniel pulled Ginny onto the dancefloor.

"I told you." She held onto him tight as they let the music move them.

He pulled her snug against his chest and dipped her low. "After this, I'm taking you out to the docks."

"Why's that?" Ginny murmured breathless.

"The moon is full, and you once told me you liked swimming by moonlight." He shrugged as he spun her, pressing her back to his chest.

"Something about that Mississippi in the moonshine just makes me want to misbehave," Ginny teased him, grinding her backside against him.

He spun her around and held her close. "I have a feeling I may regret the day I ran into you on the docks, river rat."

"The feeling is mutual."

Nathaniel kissed her in the middle of the dancefloor, and Ginny's heart sang.

EPILOGUE

Baton Rouge, Louisiana
December 1933

Nathaniel opened the car door, and Virginia stepped out onto the busy street. She fidgeted with her wrap as they approached a large brick building with tinted display windows. The air had cooled a bit, but when she shivered, it wasn't because of the cold. Her gaze drifted to Nathaniel, and she smiled.

"What are we doing here?" she asked, eyeing the storefront before glancing at the neighboring shops.

"Celebrating." Nathaniel held the front door open and motioned for her to enter.

She stepped inside and froze to the spot.

The punched tin ceilings reflected the soft light glowing from the delicate deco chandeliers. A long mahogany bar lined the wall leading to a stage tucked in the back framed with rich velvet curtains and gilded shell recessed lights. A small dancefloor lay before the stage. The tables and chairs polished and ready for awaiting customers. Neat, tidy rows of liquor lined the shelves behind the bar.

"Nathaniel." Ginny turned to him in alarm. "What if the feds show up? They'll finally have their reason to lock you away."

He offered a secret smile before pulling her into his arms.

"Don't spoil the moment," he whispered before kissing her gently. She melted against him. "We're supposed to be celebrating."

"Celebrating what?"

"The repeal of the 18th Amendment."

Ginny thought for a second before it registered in her mind. "It's over? Really?"

Nathaniel nodded. "I heard from Evans this morning. As of this moment, the sale of alcohol is no longer illegal."

"Then—" Ginny's gaze drifted past his amused expression and landed on the bar behind him where a bottle of French champagne sat in a silver bucket of ice.

"The Nightingale opens tonight." He turned and opened the bubbly, pouring two glasses. "I want you on the stage wearing that gown Pamela put you in the first night you sang at the Casa de Luna."

"I might be able to arrange that." Ginny smirked. "Any specific song you want me to open with?"

"*You're Getting to be a Habit With Me.*"

"The feeling is mutual," Ginny teased as she raised her glass. "So long, prohibition."

"To you." Nathaniel's sincere smile tugged at her heart.

The fizz tickled her nose, sending the alcohol straight to her head. Ginny chuckled. "I don't think I've ever had champagne." She tasted it again.

"Do you not like it?" he asked over the rim of his glass.

"I prefer the shine better, or your whisky." Ginny drained the rest of the bubbly liquid and sighed. "Speaking of Pamela, have you heard from her?"

"She's back in town now. I'm sure she'll be at the grand opening tonight."

"You never told me what happened after they left on the *Mississippi Queen* that night."

She watched him with interest. Every time she brought it up, he found a way to change the subject. This time she'd get the truth from him if she had to seduce him to get it.

Nathaniel sighed when she toyed with his lapel, gently sliding her hand across his vest. "He escaped."

"What?"

"Apparently after we were well on our way to see your

brothers in Alton, Levi jumped ship. Haven't seen hide nor hair of him since then." He smoothed a stray curl behind her ear. "I'm surprised Pamela hasn't found him yet."

"So that's where she's been? Hunting Levi." Ginny stifled the urge to laugh at the image that popped into her head.

"Yes...and not at my request, either. If that bastard shows up at my door, he'll get what's due, but I'm not going to waste any time or money on that traitor."

"I guess I'm still confused. Why did he turn you over to the Garretts?"

"Levi always had a love for cards, but he had horrible luck. Evans told me all his debts had been bought up by the Garrett brothers, who used it as leverage to get to me." He ran his hand through his hair. "I'd bailed him out in the past and told him I wouldn't do it anymore. I guess he thought he had to hide it."

Ginny nodded, finally understanding the pain in Levi's eyes that night, the indecision. "And Pamela, what reason would she have to keep searching for him?"

"Those two have a history. Pamela and Levi were childhood sweethearts. When he left for the war, she moved to Louisiana...in part to forget him and to start over."

"Why?"

"Because she found out she was pregnant after he'd shipped off."

Ginny gaped at Nathaniel. "She's got a kid?"

Nathaniel shook his head. "She lost the baby when she got to Baton Rouge. The place she'd been staying kicked her out, so she started working at a brothel downtown to keep her head above water. Once she'd saved up enough money, she invested in her own business. High class companionship for high class clientele."

The information sank into her mind, and Ginny saw Pamela in a whole new light. Her heart ached for her friend, but surged with pride at how well she'd done for herself.

"Does Levi know?" Ginny noted the lines marring Nathaniel's brow.

"No, and up until the night he turned traitor, they refused to spend any time in each other's company. He was sore at her for not waiting for him, and she...well, you get the gist of it."

"I can only imagine."

Nathaniel pulled her into his arms again and kissed the top of her head. "I just hope she doesn't kill him when she finds him."

"Why's that?" Ginny asked, meeting his gaze. "I thought you didn't care what happened to him."

"I don't," Nathaniel replied. "I'd just like a few answers before she pulls the trigger."

"Don't start acting like you're a cold-hearted gangster now." Ginny straightened his tie. "You're a legitimate businessman."

He offered his arm. "Shall we go then? I'll have them finish preparations for tonight while you and I tie up some loose ends at de Luna."

"I hope you're implying something altogether inappropriate, Nathaniel." Ginny winked at him.

"Of course, now that it's legal to indulge, I've gotta appease my sinful nature somehow." He kissed her soundly before ushering her out into the December morning air.

THE END

OTHER BOOKS BY KIRSTEN S. BLACKETER

CRAVING 1985 SERIES

When I Found You
Can't Fight This Feeling
She Gives Love a Bad Name
Owner of a Lonely Heart
Just What I Needed

HISTORICAL

An Irresistible Shadow
A Shadow's Kiss
Mississippi Moonshine
Deceiving the Earl
Jewel of Winter
At Winter's Demand
Under Winter's Control
Seducing Winter's Gentleman
Stealing the Widow's Heart
Seduction on the Alpine Express
Temptation on the Alpine Express

CONTEMPORARY

A Lockdown Love Affair
A Holiday Love Affair
Mistletoe and Mistakes
Confessions of a Fangirl
Confessions of a Gamer Girl
Confessions of a Glamour Girl
The Flight Before Christmas

FANTASY/FAIRYTALE

Curse of the Huntsman's Jewel
The Huntsman's Revenge

PIRATES AND PERSUASION

Queen Takes Hook

ABOUT THE AUTHOR

Kirsten S. Blacketer is a multi-published indie author of both historical and contemporary romance. When she's not writing, she homeschools her two children and enjoys time with her family. In those moments of freedom, she devours romance novels while sipping a glass of wine. Age has only shown her that writing villains can be just as fun as heroes. Her next life goals are to write a New York Times Bestseller and one day have Adam Driver play a starring role in a film version of one of her books. A girl can dream, right?

Read more at **http://kirstensblacketer.com.**

ALSO WRITES AS JEN BRADLEE